THE LURKING MAN

SHADE OF THE REAPER SERIES

KEITH ROMMEL

MILFORD HOUSE

an imprint of Sunbury Press, Inc.
Mechanicsburg, PA USA

MILFORD HOUSE

an imprint of Sunbury Press, Inc.
Mechanicsburg, PA USA

For information about special discounts for bulk purchases, please contact Sunbury Press Orders Dept. at (855) 338-8359 or orders@sunburypress.com.

To request one of our authors for speaking engagements or book signings, please contact Sunbury Press Publicity Dept. at publicity@sunburypress.com.

SECOND MILFORD HOUSE PRESS EDITION: October 2025

Set in Adobe Garamond | Interior design by Crystal Devine | Cover design by Lawrence Knorr | Edited by Jennifer Cappello | Cover images used with permission. RMR Productions. Daniel Lench as Sariel, Tessa Espinola as young Cailean and Maritza Brikisak as Cailean.

Publisher's Cataloging-in-Publication Data
Names: Rommel, Keith, author.
Title: The lurking man / Keith Rommel.
Description: First trade paperback edition. | Mechanicsburg, PA : Milford House Press, 2025.
Summary: A supernatural entity suspends a troubled woman in limbo, forcing her to relive the sins of her past.
Identifiers: ISBN : 978-1-62006-440-5 (softcover).
Subjects: FICTION / Thrillers / Psychological | FICTION / Psychological.

Designed in the USA
0 1 1 2 3 5 8 13 21 34 55

For the Love of Books!

1

CIRCLE OF HELL

Present day.

"Who are you and what am I doing here?" Cailean said, and stared at the thick, impenetrable wall of darkness that surrounded her. She tried to focus on something that moved inside the blackness.

A single spotlight that hung overhead encased her in a perfect circle of blinding luminescence. She stepped forward and was careful not to touch the obscurity. Something about it made her cautious.

"I demand that you come closer so I can see you!"

Absolute silence greeted her like a defiant slap to the face.

She cupped her hands around her mouth, drew a deep breath, stood on her toes, and shouted, "Now, you son of a bitch!"

Vapor from her breath swirled in the unnatural light and she coughed from the strain on her throat.

Snow started to fall and flakes spun around her in a graceful, mesmerizing dance.

"I know you're there," she said, and paused to allow her senses to work. Just outside the distinct edge of light she could hear faint movement. The flesh on her arms goosed and she resisted the desire to back away. "Tell me what this is about. I deserve to know!"

The snow fell harder and a powerful wind blasted it sideways. It pelted her face and forced her eyes away. The feeling of something that was close and evil terrified her. But the idea that it toyed with her fueled her temper. She clenched her fists and bared her teeth.

"Is this how you get your thrills, by scaring women?"

An intensifying tangle of white distorted her perception and the overhead light made her feel that much more vulnerable.

"I am not afraid of you," she said, and no matter how loudly or sternly she shouted those words, she knew how weak and unbelievable they really were.

A deep, menacing chuckle filled the lighted space and she hurried to the center of the brightness. She defied the battering onslaught of powerful squalls and tried to conceal her crumbling composure.

"I don't see what is funny about this. What are you laughing at?"

The laughter faded and the storm tapered off as if it were a calmed response to her outrage. The moment of silence that followed exposed the crack in Cailean's armor. She was alone, unarmed, and only had her fear and confusion to accompany her.

But yet the fading echo of his laughter reminded her that she was not alone in this place. There was something beyond the light that stalked her, preyed upon her, and all she wanted to do was run and hide, but she had nowhere to go. She was trapped in a ten-foot perfect circle with knee-high snow, wearing nothing but a turtleneck sweater, boots, and a pair of worn blue jeans.

"Please," she said.

The sound of snow crunching underfoot diverted her attention. But the noise—like the laughter—seemed to come from everywhere but nowhere in particular.

"What do you want from me?" she said, panicked, as she continued to look all around. The shadows morphed and moved and gave her the impression that there was more than one of them beyond the light.

"Your life," he said, and the sound of his voice was like a sudden crack of thunder that made her flinch. Deep and disturbing, it carried an ominous tone that filled her with certain dread.

"Who are you?" she said again, and turned around fast to see if he stood behind her.

"I am someone beyond your understanding."

His whereabouts were confusing and she looked elsewhere with frantic, indecisive movement. Instinct told her to stay inside the light, that it would keep her safe.

"Why am I here?" she said. "And why do you hide in the dark?"

The sensation of being watched by that thing with nothing to hide behind made her feel unclean.

"I want to know why you hide in the dark!"

"The darkness is where I dwell," he said. "Come, I want you to see what true darkness is like."

She stiffened, but fought against her abnegation and took a step forward to prove her bravery. "No, I won't go where you are, I'm not stupid. Besides, I haven't seen you, and if you let me go I won't tell anyone about this."

A thunderous, diabolical laughter exploded all around her, and before it faded away, the hideous bellow of his gravelly voice bore down on her.

"There is nothing for you to tell. Everyone knows of me, but they know so little about me. And where you are now is a place you can't walk away from. I have brought you here for a purpose and it starts with my stripping you of all your excuses and exposing you for who you really were."

"For who I was? What do you claim to know about me?"

The silence came again and it was intrusive and heavy. Cailean had a need to fill the void but struggled to find the words. Instead, she tugged on her sweater and brushed away the snow that clung to her. She bunched the sleeves into the palms of her hands and folded her arms across her chest.

"You don't know me," she said.

"I know more about you than anyone, even you. Although I am from the darkness, I will bring your truth to light and I will expose you."

His words were vexing.

"Now tell me," he said. "What is the last thing you remember?"

She licked her lips and descended deep into the archives of her mind. She searched aimlessly for the answer to his question, but the farther she went in, the farther away the answer seemed to be.

"I asked you, what was the last thing you remember?" the foul voice roared.

Ripped from her reverie she came out with nothing. "I don't know! Being here, standing underneath this damn light, sensing you all around me, and then the snow." She panted and a small puff of vapor escaped her mouth and barely stained the air. "I don't know how I knew, but I did. I knew you were around, watching me. It was like I could feel you."

A gentle chuckle came again and lingered with an ongoing echo. "That's because we have met before, several times. You've had my attention since you were a young lady. I admire you for being so brave in the face of such tragedy."

His words were tied to no memory of hers and meant nothing. She checked her position within the light, and said, "I don't know what that is supposed to mean. I've already told you that I can't remember a thing beyond waking up here underneath the light."

"It will come to you, all of it. And it will make you appreciate this moment. I know what is said about ignorance and you will soon know that it is true. This moment is going to be the easiest of your time here because denial, anger, and blame will try to interfere with your ability to come to terms with who you were."

"Who sent you?"

"I am not sent, I come."

"Who are you?"

"I am everyone's fear and wonder, ultimate desire and destination."

"Stop it!" she said. "You speak in riddles as if this is some sort of a game to you. I demand to know what this is about!"

"I take demands from no one, and here, I obey no one."

"You hide in the dark like a coward!"

"And you have made many horrible choices in your life, Cailean, and for that reason I have no sympathy for you."

She ran a hand through her hair and came out with a fistful of snow. Suddenly the man beyond the light and the things he said didn't matter anymore.

"You have affected people close to you in ways you could never imagine," he said.

"What is happening to me?"

"Now I have your attention?"

She fell to her knees in a powdery drift of snow and pushed her hands into the mound.

"Why can't I feel the cold?"

"You threw your life away so long ago and now you ask what happened to it?" he said.

She looked at the bleak partition. It was a wall of pitch-black nothingness that held many secrets.

"Something is wrong with me."

"Yes," he said. "Something has been wrong with you for a long time."

She returned her attention to her hands. "Why can't I feel them?"

The snowfall came again hard and fast; this time it created a whiteout.

"You need to calm yourself," he said. "Your emotions are a tempest of confusion and can cause us great delays. You have a tough decision to make and it is going to require a sound mind. We have much to talk about and you will need to follow my instructions exactly as I give them. Now gather yourself and sit down at the table behind you."

Cailean looked, and as the voice had said, a table and two chairs were behind her, covered in snow. She pushed herself to her feet, perplexed; she hadn't noticed the furniture until now. She brushed the snow off of one of the chairs.

"You are in a large room with a door at either end," he said. "Each door has a different fate for you. I am going to help you remember the decisions of your life, and once you have seen it all, I am going to ask you to choose which door you prefer."

"What are you talking about? What door?" Cailean lifted a hand to fend off the continuous barrage of frozen pellets that obscured her vision. She scanned the white wall and wept. "I can't see a damn thing. How am I supposed to know which door to choose?"

She sat heavily in the chair.

The quiet reigned, and with it, the snowfall thinned off. She stopped crying and her eyes widened as they swept over the pasty silhouette of a tall shadow man standing hunched at the edge of the black veil. He appeared darker than anything she had ever seen before—even the denseness outside the light she occupied.

"Who are you? And why don't you come closer so I can see you?" she said, and mopped her eyes with the back of her hand.

"I've told you that the darkness is where I dwell. Besides, if you were to see me for what I am—"

"For what you are? What is that supposed to mean?" She stood up, took a few steps forward and tried to make out specifics. His form held many secrets and appeared as a stain on the blackness.

"Sit back down," he said. "We have much to consider."

Cailean looked at the chair and then back at the shadow man. "I'm not going to sit until you tell me what this is about!" she said, and grunted. She staggered backwards and fell into the chair.

"Did you do that to me?" she said, her eyes wide with surprise. She could feel where the hands had shoved her. "Did you just push me?"

"I will do what must be done to get you to follow my instructions while you are here. So much depends on it."

She looked all around her, and to her dismay, she was certain that she alone occupied the light. There was no trace of him entering or leaving the circle.

"Please," she said and continued to look here and there. She slid to the edge of her seat and worry softened her expression. "I just want to know what this is about."

The man remained motionless at the edge of the light. And although hidden, she could feel his piercing stare.

"I need you to look at the light over your head," he said.

Cailean thought to defy him, but she remembered the force behind the shove and her uncertainty as to how he had done that. She looked at the light.

"Now, exhale," he said.

Unsure what this would prove, she drew a deep breath and exhaled. No vapor formed and she did it again with the same result. Her eyes widened and she jumped to her feet. "Please, I'm scared!" she said, and moved towards the shadow man. He retreated into the darkness.

"Cailean," he said. "You are dead to the world you know and I am the one who brings death to the people. I am called Sariel, and I've brought you here, to an aperture. It's a place I've created especially for you, and it is located between the living and the dead. I've brought you here to show you the sins of your past and to offer you a chance at redemption."

2

GUILTY CONSCIENCE

The past.

"Look out your window and tell me what you see," Cailean said into the telephone.

"I know what it is doing outside, Cailean. Besides, I wouldn't need to look, because no matter what is happening out there, I'm sure there is enough going on for you to make up ten excuses as to why you can't come," Wilson said.

"You do realize it's snowing like crazy and the roads are completely covered, don't you?"

"I really tried to believe that I wasn't going to get this phone call from you today, I really did. But deep down inside I knew it was coming because I know you and the way you are."

"The way I am?" she said. "What is that supposed to mean?"

"You know exactly what it means. Beau and I have been played the fool for the last time."

"Stop being such an ass, Wilson. Think about why you're getting so mad, it's stupid. Do you really think it's safe for me to drive him around in this?"

"I'm not a child that hasn't seen his mother in over a month," he said. "So I don't think it really matters what I think. You're hurting your son again and you can't even see it."

"There are severe weather warnings all over the news. My not wanting to drive him around in this is my showing him that I care."

"We've been through it enough times that I know what you're doing," he said.

"Tell me, what am I doing?"

"You have your perfect excuse and you won't let it go."

"Is that what I'm doing?"

"Why don't you just get it over with and say that you don't want to see him?"

"No, I'm not going to say that. I want you to stop putting words in my mouth."

"I'm just stating what is obvious," he said.

"I can't believe the things I am hearing out of you. You, the overprotective father of the year, are encouraging me to take his son out in this?"

"He's your son, too. If you would have showed up like you were supposed to, I was going to suggest that you stayed here with him. I was going to go to the other side of the house so you could have your privacy. You wouldn't even know I was there."

"I would know," she said, the words oozed with indifference.

"You need to get over it and move on for Beau's sake."

"There is no way I could step foot in that house again. It's just not possible—especially under the circumstances that I was forced to leave."

"What other choice did I have?" he said.

The long silence that followed was crammed with unresolved issues and private anger.

"Listen, Cailean, it wasn't my intention to get into it with you," Wilson said. "I just want you to know that every time you're supposed to come for him it seems like there is always an excuse at your disposal."

"So what are you saying, now I have control over the weather?"

"No, that's not what I'm saying at all. Two weeks ago you canceled because you said it was raining too hard. A week before that it was a fog or something. I really don't remember and I can't keep track anymore."

"It was like a monsoon outside and you know it. I drove a few blocks and couldn't see five feet in front of my face."

"I don't think a waterfall and all of the snow in the world could keep me from seeing my son."

"Good for you! You're perfect in every way and I am damaged and should be discarded like a piece of trash," she said.

"I hope you understand that all of these excuses as to why you can't come don't mean a thing to him. The only thing he wants is to see you and to feel loved by you. I refuse to tell him that you're not coming again.

I won't break his heart and spend the next week trying to repair it. Too many times I've had to tell him that he didn't do anything wrong and that he doesn't deserve to be treated that way. Not by you or anyone else."

Cailean walked to the window and pulled the shade aside. Everything was covered in a six-inch blanket of snow. Ice wrapped sagging power lines and coated the trees in a heavy crystallized blanket. Snowflakes filled the air, encouraged by a beating wind.

"For crying out loud, Wilson, what the hell do you want me to do? We're in the middle of a blizzard!"

"He's been dressed for over two hours and all he can talk about is seeing you." He laughed. "You should have heard him yesterday. He must have asked me fifty times if you were coming and every time I told him yes, his eyes would light up and he'd have this great big smile take over his face."

She sighed and looked at the ceiling. "Hey, God, shut the damn storm off would you? I've got to go pick up my son and I don't want to get killed in the process."

"Stop acting so foolish, Cailean. If you're not coming, then you're going to be the one who is going to tell him, not me. I want you to listen to the disappointment in his voice so you can carry that around with you like I do."

"You can be such a bastard. I carry enough crap around with me and you know it."

Wilson breathed into the phone.

"Sadly, I've come to realize that most of it has been your own doing," he said.

"Is that what you think?"

"I'm not going to debate this anymore because it's merely my opinion. Now, would you like me to put him on the phone?"

"You don't think anything I went through as a kid had to do with it? You can be so infuriating, Wilson."

"I said I'm not going to debate it," he said.

Indecipherable noise came through the phone.

"Beau, your mother would like to speak to you!"

"Don't you dare do that, Wilson. I'll hang up on you!"

"Go ahead and hang up then!"

She visualized everything Wilson had said, and as frustrating as it was, she knew every word of it was probably true. "No, I don't want to do that," she said, and flicked the shade away. She lowered her voice to a whisper. "Go ahead; make me look like the bad guy in all of this."

"This isn't about you or me and how we feel about each other," Wilson said. "This is about Beau."

Cailean rolled her eyes and fought against her frustration. The games Wilson played on her emotions were becoming tiresome, and the way he used Beau as a weapon was nothing short of infuriating.

"I know what you're trying to do," she said.

"What are you talking about?"

"You're trying to manipulate me into feeling bad so I conform to your will."

"Please, Cailean, not this . . ."

"I know you're doing it so I come. It is how you try and show your control over me."

"I have never tried to control you, not once."

"You have to stop thinking I am around for you to use as your doormat."

"The way I see it, Beau and I are the doormats. We haven't seen you for the better part of a month," Wilson said. "And every time you're supposed to come, you don't. I often wish you never stopped attending your therapy sessions. You have some serious problems . . . you just can't see it. I often wonder what our marriage would have been like if you would have stayed the course."

"Our marriage was a disaster and you know it. And you need to know that I'm not a science project. I'm a person with real feelings that grew up in terrible tragedy."

"I know that," he said, and the dissatisfaction of having to live with that fact seeped through the phone. "Listen, I don't want to keep going around in circles about this. I just want you to know that he misses you—that's all. He's questioned if he is the reason you left. It's hurtful to hear him ask these types of questions over and over again. I'm sure we can at least agree that he doesn't deserve that."

Cailean clamped her eyes shut and rubbed her temples. "I can't do this, not now. I need a little time to think about the things that were just said."

"What is there to think about?"

"This hasn't been our best moment."

"You see? You just don't get it. Just tell me when it becomes about Beau being first."

"Look, I need to hang up the phone now and I'm going to have to call you back," she said.

"I don't understand why."

"That's part of the reason why I left without much of a fight. You never understood."

"And that's the reason why I needed to let you go. You wear that day, that horrible event, like ten-ton shackles that bind your very soul. You've allowed it to strip the compassion right out of you. And the biggest problem is that everyone around you suffers for it, too. No matter how much they love you, they can't escape the ghosts of your past. But it's like I said, it's not about either one of us anymore and I'm not trying to turn it into that. So, what should we do about Beau?"

"Nothing," she said. "I don't want to tell him anything yet. I need to figure some things out and I'll call you back when I can."

"Please tell me you're not going to have a drink. You know as well as I do that you're not going to find any answers there."

Cailean ignored what he said and jabbed a finger into the off button on the phone. She spun on her heels and plopped down on the plush couch. She tossed the phone aside, grabbed her top lip with her teeth, and shook her head. "What a jerk. I can't believe I married him."

An electronic picture frame on the end table she hadn't noticed until now displayed a new photograph that grabbed Cailean's attention. She and Beau sat close; their heads were tilted and their smiles were wide. They both wore baseball caps, and the sun was so bright that day that it made them both squint.

Cailean picked up the picture frame and placed it on her lap. She studied it for a moment longer and touched Beau's image.

An otherwise suppressed smile parted her lips and her eyes welled with tears. She resisted and quickly erected self-control.

"Yeah," she said and gave a sullen nod. "How could I ever forget that day?"

The park; the one with the big blue curly slide next to the river. The boats that sped by and created a wake that lapped the big rocks on the shore. She loved that sound but couldn't hear that soothing swish anymore. All she could hear were the terrified screams from people she didn't know.

The picture fizzled and a beautiful sunset with a seagull that rode the breeze came into frame.

Cailean rubbed her eyes and shut off the picture frame. She placed it on the couch beside her, and with a sigh, she stood.

"Yeah, that's just great, something else to add to my guilt."

She mulled over the exchange she just had with Wilson while she walked up a flight of wooden steps that bowed and creaked under her weight.

"I can never win," she said, and entered the bedroom. Emerson was on his back with his head propped up on a mound of pillows. He sipped wine and watched courtroom television.

"Hey," he said, and flashed a smile.

"Hey," she said, and didn't feel like returning the gesture. She really didn't want to look at him right now let alone have him in her bed.

"Are you OK?" he said.

She tried to ignore the wine bottle and the full snifter glass that waited for her on the nightstand. "I'm feeling a little guilty right now," she said, and sat heavily on the edge of the bed with her back to him. "Were you listening to the phone conversation?"

"Yeah, I heard some of it."

"Did you put that picture thing out? The one of me and Beau at the park?"

"Yeah, I put it out there last night after you fell asleep. I was trying to surprise you."

He came up behind her and kissed her neck. She moved away, unable to hide her indifference to his touch.

"You've been talking about him a lot lately," he said, and ignored her reaction. "You refuse to decorate and everything is so bare inside here that I wanted to try and brighten the room and make it feel like a home. I figured I would start with something small that had significant meaning to you. I hope you're not upset about it."

"Where did you get it from?"

"I bought it," he said. "I downloaded the pictures from my computer at home."

"I didn't even know you had that picture anymore. I forgot about it and would have preferred it to stay that way. The timing of it was all wrong."

She hung her head and breathed. The smell of the wine on his breath roused her desire for some.

"I'm sorry, I just thought—"

Cailean waved a hand. "Yeah, I get that. It's just—"

"I'll take the frame away."

"No, don't. You're right. There's not a single picture throughout the entire house and it is time we added some life to it. I think I'm a little sensitive right now and I'm taking my frustrations out on you. It's just that Wilson and Beau . . ."

She fell into a silence filled with a hundred different possibilities.

"Ah, just forget it, it really doesn't matter," she said.

"Yes it does! You need to talk about what you're feeling and stop bottling everything up."

"No I really don't. I said to forget it."

"Well, for the record he is a pain in the ass, Cailean. You know that?"

She glared at Emerson.

"I'm talking about Wilson," he said. "Beau is a great kid."

Cailean smiled. "Yeah, he is a great kid, and Wilson *is* a pain in the ass." She laughed but quickly turned serious. "I suppose there is nothing more frustrating than finding out that you're the inadequate parent over and over again."

"You're not inadequate and he is no better than you."

"I know why you're saying that and I can even appreciate it, but the truth is Wilson is the better parent. I don't trust myself with Beau anymore than I would some stranger off the streets. There is no denying that I've caused him a lot of harm."

Emerson scooted to the edge of the bed and sat close to Cailean.

"Why do you allow him to do this to you?"

Cailean shrugged and a tear fell from her eye. Maybe she was giving in to Wilson's manipulation and needed assistance. She looked at the nightstand and stared at the bottle of wine. Just one drink could go a long way in helping taking some of the edge off.

"I guess some truths are hard to accept," she said. "Especially when you're hung over and slinging any excuse you can find because it's the easy thing to do." She shook her head. "I don't know, but seeing that picture right afterwards was like a dagger to my heart."

"I'm sorry, that's not why I put it there. I'll take it away."

"And I said not to! I need you to listen to me. Wilson never did and that drove me absolutely nuts."

"OK, I heard you. I'm sorry."

"I think I need to see that picture, and as strange as it might sound right now, I think I needed to hear what Wilson had to say. You know as well as I do that there is a whole bunch of truth in his words."

"You're allowing him to do it again," Emerson said and put his arm around her. "You're better than that. And I put that frame out there to bring you joy—not to hurt you in any way."

Cailean bobbed her head and wiped her eyes. She slithered out of his grasp. "I know, and I appreciate that." She patted his thick, calloused hand and stood. "It was really nice of you to do that, thank you."

She picked her jeans up off the floor, shook them out, and started to dress.

"Are you going somewhere?"

"I have to get Beau. It's the right thing for me to do."

"I don't think it's a good idea. It's really bad out there, Cailean."

"I know it is, and I've already told Wilson that. It doesn't matter to him in the least."

"It does to me and I think you should call him back and let him know you're going to have to change it to next weekend."

"I've done that for the past three weekends." She paused and tried to remember the last time she saw Beau. "No, it has probably been a lot longer than that. Maybe like five or six weekends."

"Regardless, you can't control the weather."

"I said that, too."

Emerson got up and started to dress. "Well, the least I can do is drive you."

Cailean smiled. "Very noble, but no." She pulled a shirt over her head and fixed it properly around her waist. "Things are still too fresh between Wilson and me. It's bad enough Beau blames me for what's going on already. I don't need to add insult to injury by bringing my boyfriend with me. Especially you."

"Especially me? What is that supposed to mean?"

"Exactly what it sounds like, Emerson. Can you really blame Wilson for not liking you?"

"I didn't do anything to him. And besides, it's not like Wilson doesn't know about us."

"Of course he knows, but Beau doesn't and I would prefer it to stay that way. Besides, like it or not, Wilson and I are still married."

Emerson scowled.

Cailean squared her shoulders and fixed Emerson with a stern look. "We are still married, and there is a young boy caught in the middle of this mess. I think he's been through enough, don't you?"

Emerson rolled his eyes and looked away.

"Oh please, Emerson, it's time to grow up."

His eyes went wide. "I don't know why you let him get inside your head." He tapped his temple and took a drink. "He crawls around inside there and rearranges things on you. I swear he makes you crazy."

"I feel like that's what you're doing to me right now!"

"Yeah, sure." He reinforced his position with a chuckle. "The problem is that you don't let me inside. I've been knocking on a closed door and begging you to let me in. But you've got every barrel, bolt, and hasp securely locked and there's no way you're going to let me in."

"If you're alluding to my past again, I want you to know that I really don't appreciate it. I've already told you that it is something I don't want to talk about."

Emerson shook his head and looked away, his voice barely above a whisper. "You told me you were just a kid when it happened. That had to be thirty years ago. I don't understand what could be so bad."

She buttoned and zipped her jeans with attitude. "You're right. Having grown up with a silver spoon in your mouth you couldn't possibly begin to understand. Sometimes you act like a goddamn baby, you know that?"

Emerson pointed at himself. "Why are you calling me a baby?"

She pushed her feet into her dirty, worn sneakers. "Because sometimes you should just shut up and listen. Not everything I say requires a response."

He placed his drink down on a nearby dresser and pulled on his pants. "I'm sorry, maybe you're right."

"There is no maybe about it. I'm right and you're an ass."

"I just can't stand the way Wilson constantly tries to make you feel bad."

Cailean laughed and pointed at Emerson. "So, what, are you my protector or something?"

Emerson crossed his hairy arms across his flabby chest. "No, I'm not."

"Good, because I am more than capable of taking care of myself."

"Yeah, I know, you remind me of that every time you hang up the phone with him. This is really starting to get old and I'm beginning to wonder what I'm doing here."

Cailean stared at his naked chest and looked away in disgust. He had bigger boobs than she did. The things she had to do to get by were humiliating. She walked to Emerson and pointed a finger in his face. "And if you're not smart enough to figure out what you're doing here, then that sounds to me like you have a problem."

"Get your finger outta my face."

"Or what?" She slapped him hard and followed up with a shove.

Surprise caught Emerson off balance, and he backpedaled and slammed into the wall. His eyes opened wide and he brought his finger to his lip.

"You hit me!"

"You're damn right I hit you! You crowd me and say stupid things that provoke me. What do you expect me to do?"

"Not this!" He showed her the blood on his finger and licked his lips.

"I don't feel an ounce of regret because you deserved that," she said. "Now I want you to get out of my house before things get any worse between us."

3

THE SEED WITHIN

Present day.

"Cailean?" Sariel said.

The terrible voice that beckoned her from deep within the beyond distracted her. She resisted its call and tried to remain within the moment when she had told Emerson to leave.

"The events you saw, are they familiar to you?"

She nodded and tried to keep her concentration.

"Good, your awareness is much keener than I anticipated, especially this early on."

She struggled to put the pieces of her past together. The possibility that the moment she had just experienced may have very well been the last of her life troubled her.

"Why can't I remember anything further?"

"The transition from that side to this one can be difficult, especially if it comes unexpectedly."

"Did I die at that time? Was it a heart attack?"

"No, you didn't die there, and what killed you was something far worse than a heart attack."

Physically, she felt fine and had heard that when you die you don't keep any of your bodily ailments.

"What was it then?"

"You and what you were."

"I don't understand."

"In time, you will."

"What I saw then," she said, "the phone call with Wilson and the argument with Emerson, when did that happen?"

"Yesterday."

She looked upon the ebon wall, perplexed, and her care to understand anything further about the interaction she had with Emerson was simply abandoned.

"How is that possible?"

"How is it possible you have died and yet I can talk to you?"

The question dizzied her head. Her gaze drifted around the snow filled room and swept over the black veil. She tried to comprehend the idea that a full day had passed since those events had transpired when she believed it had all happened only a few seconds ago.

"Inside, that doesn't make sense to me," she said. "It just can't be right. How long have I been dead?"

"A little under a minute."

Stunned by the reply, she felt displaced. All sense of time had escaped her and she was a million miles away from knowing who she was and why she was here.

"Did you say under a minute?"

"As you measure time, yes."

Her body trembled and she felt sick.

"Don't try to fight it," he said. "The understanding of your condition and the transformation of your body will come regardless. Accept that things are different here and the only control you have now is what I give you."

"Please, I need to get out of here right now!"

"If you allow your fear to control you it will only hamper your ability to understand the things you must know about yourself in order to move on."

A powerful yearning stirred within her and validated Sariel's words. The desire to know was sudden and insatiable and it made her whimper.

"Does Wilson have anything to do with this?" she said.

A deep, diabolical giggle sent a chill down her spine and filled her with a fear so intense that it paralyzed her.

"Even in your first moments of death you still look to blame Wilson? He tried for years to save you from this because he knew whatever was inside of you was stronger than you and he feared you would never be able to escape its grasp."

The words were powerful enough to bring her to her knees. "Please," she said. "I am begging you to let me go. You're scaring me!"

The groan of the wind and the guttural sounds that accompanied Sariel's nearness distressed her.

"I'm not the bad one here, Cailean, you are. I'm the one who should be afraid of you."

"You're not the one trapped underneath a light being studied like a lab rat."

"You did that to everyone you knew. Wilson, Beau, and even Emerson were merely pieces to a complex puzzle you fit together to help justify your lies and feed your addictions. The first tragedy in your life combined with the second made the outcome of the third unavoidable. That is what brought you here."

Her head hurt and everything about the moment didn't seem real. She wanted to wake up from this dreadful dream, but the overhead light and snow remained firmly in place.

"I want to get out of here in the worst way, but I can't."

"Why?"

"I don't know!"

"It may not make any sense to you, but you know."

"I have a need to understand what those events were."

He tittered. "I told you that you knew. What you find, the things you will unearth, it is going to change you in ways you could never imagine."

A shiver rocked her body and she brushed at something unseen on her arms.

"Who is there with you?" she said, and looked here and there to try to figure things out. "I feel judging eyes on me like bugs crawling on my skin."

"There is no one else here. I am alone with you."

She worked harder to escape the feeling, frantic in her every movement.

"Why do I doubt what you are saying to me is the truth? There have to be more people with you, I can feel them."

"Cailean?"

His beckoning chased the sensation away and she focused on his voice.

"It is just us here," he said.

The lurid tone was something out of a nightmare.

The snow filled the air again, but oddly it defied all sense of logic and lifted from the ground and went upwards. She watched the bizarre happening and it helped draw her attention away from all the things that troubled her only a moment ago.

Up above, past the light, a thick black canopy loomed overhead and threatened to press down on her. She felt pathetic and small and she imagined being an ant underneath the treads of a shoe.

The sensation of a thousand pinpricks consumed the flesh on her hands and she growled at the sudden strange feelings. She flexed her fingers and studied them with intense scrutiny. They were losing their normal fleshy tone and turning white.

"You are shedding the senses of your human body and you're in the beginning stages of adapting to your new form. The doctors are delaying this as they try and save your life. Your body goes into full cardiac arrest on the other side and they bring you back."

"No," she said and shook her hands in an attempt to dislodge the feeling.

Sariel giggled ever so gently. "Oh yes, it will consume your body soon, and when it does there is no going back. Do you wish to stop it?"

She stepped forward, hopeful. "Is there a way?"

"Study the details of your life and consider my offer," he said.

"I want you to tell me everything I need to know so I can accept whatever it is you want so you can make this stop."

"No," he said. "There are no shortcuts. You must understand what your life decisions were so you can make a choice absent of fear and desperation."

"Why? I already know that I don't want to feel the way I'm feeling now. I'll do it, whatever it is you need, just make this stop."

"It cannot be done that way."

"This lesson is pointless when you have told me I will despise who I was."

"This lesson means everything," he said. "What I am going to ask of you in exchange is inconceivable. We have this one chance only, and once you either accept or deny my offer it cannot be undone."

His foreboding stifled her desire to inquire further. Filled with worry, she flexed her hands, and although she had full motion and total coordination, she couldn't feel her fingertips when they touched her palms.

She walked the perimeter of light, moving dangerously close to the inky partition. While she attempted to contemplate the grievous situation she found herself in, jumbled, pushy voices interrupted her reverie.

"What?" she said and stopped to listen. "What did you just say?"

"What is it you hear, Cailean?"

She didn't want to say it but suspected he might know. "People are accusing me of horrible things! I thought you said we were alone!"

"We are."

The voices and their words became distinct and they came from all around.

"No," she said. "We're not! I can hear them speaking right now!"

"What are they telling you?"

She covered her ears. "That I was a horrible mother, wife, and person. They say I was selfish, an abuser, and a drunk."

Her hands were forced from her head and pushed to her sides.

"What you're hearing are thoughts from others close to you. Defend yourself against the accusations if they are untrue."

"I can't," she said, defeated. "I can't remember a damn thing."

The voices stopped.

"Because everything they've said to you are truths."

"How am I supposed to know that?"

"Because I know what's inside of you and what has made you tick."

The intemperate weather conditions continued to worsen and work on her patience. How could she be expected to stave off accusations when she lacked knowledge? And what if she were to demand the question and just guess at the door?

Although the idea was enticing, she submitted to the fact that taking a guess wouldn't be possible. She wanted out of the storm, out from underneath the light, and away from the creature in the dark that stalked her like a buzzard waiting for her to drop. But no matter how frustrated she became, her need to know how she got trapped in a ten-foot circle with her own hell lurking around in the dark prevailed.

"How long am I going to have to endure this?" she said.

"You have yet to endure anything. You are still ignorant and are merely consumed with a persistent desire to know. But when all things come together and you start to understand, that's when you will be tested."

His words were infuriating and her composure began to break down. She needed something, anything to keep from having to face them.

"What about this light and the damn snow and its unrelenting barrage?" she said. "It's chaos here and it's driving me crazy. The blackness that surrounds me is like a living cage. How long will I have to tolerate it staring back at me as if I was this horrible person as you and those voices have claimed me to be?"

"For as long as it takes."

The answer was provoking and a sudden anger coursed through her body.

"And what if I refuse to go along?" she said, forgetting her trepidation. "What will you do, push me around and keep me trapped?"

The snow stopped instantly and the quiet reminded her of her fear. It came into her body through her head and feet and occupied her chest.

Right in front of Cailean, a fist emerged out of the darkness and into the light, moving slowly and precisely. The wrinkly white, age spot-dotted skin shimmered, and long, thick fingers unfolded. Lengthy, tangled fingernails held her gaze.

"Come closer," Sariel said, and wiggled a gesturing finger. The fingernails scraped together and sounded like the squeak of tree branch swaying in a battering storm. The way the light reflected off of his skin made her squint and she remained still, rendered immobile by what she saw.

"Take my hand and I will leave you as you are," he said. "You will not have to worry about the overhead light, snow, or your confusion. The only thing you will have to look forward to is your judgment."

She clasped her hands behind her back and stepped far enough away that she was out of his reach. "As much as I want to, as enticing as your offer is, I cannot."

"No," Sariel said. "You couldn't even if you wanted to. The moment I brought you here I planted a seed of curiosity in the essence of your very being. The constant longing of trying to understand who you are will continue to grow and consume you. And if you don't find answers here you will never know because I am the only one that can help you."

For Cailean, there was no denying that there were many unanswered questions that needed resolution before she could move on. What was it about the picture of Beau in the park that caused her such distress? And what had she done to her son that consumed her with such self-hatred and guilt? And what were the three events that Sariel had said shaped her life?

"You are right," she said, and turned her back. "I understand that the answers I seek are here, underneath this light. And although I am unhappy here, I am as you suggest—at your mercy."

The low, raspy wheeze of his breathing remained undisturbed and near as he seemed to contemplate her surrender.

"Very well," Sariel said, and withdrew his hand.

And with that, the sound of snow that crunched underfoot moved away from the light and the darkness progressively deepened.

Bang!

Cailean shrieked at the sudden noise, and in unison, the circle of light she stood in expanded by a full two feet. She spun around, confounded by what she saw.

The snow was packed tight where the edge of darkness had receded. Sariel's colossal footprints were parallel to Cailean's and she remained focused on that. They walked the border of light and dark at an arm's distance away from each other.

"My God," Cailean said with her mouth agape.

4

ONE MORE DRINK

The past.

"Why do I feel like I'm always defending myself?" Emerson said.

"I'm warning you, you should just leave."

"I pay the rent!"

"I could care less what you pay for, Emerson. I live here, not you."

"My name is on the lease, Cailean. I have as much right to be here as you."

"You think so?"

"Yes, I do."

"I don't think you want to play that game with me. The way I see things from here is that you are stuck with the bill. I'll bust up the house, crap in all the corners, and it will take you months to have me evicted."

"Why are you talking like that? I wouldn't evict you and you know it. I'd pay the rent for as long as you needed."

"So why are you arguing the point that I've asked you to leave? Not that it wasn't nice of you to get me a roof over my head, but you have me stuffed in this small condo and I can't get away from you if I tried. I swear, I feel like you picked this place on purpose so you could watch my every move."

"That's ridiculous!"

"Well, it seems ridiculous that you're fighting with me because I'm looking for a little bit of space to try and figure things out."

"What am I supposed to do?"

"Leave me alone!" she said. "That's it. Just leave me alone when I ask."

"I can't, not when things are like this. I don't even understand why your anger is directed towards me when I thought we were having a meaningful conversation."

"Really, Emerson? I've had enough stress for one day and if you're not going to leave, then I will."

"You don't have to leave."

"I don't care if I have to sleep in my damn car. All I'm asking for is a little space so I can clear my head."

"OK," Emerson said. "Let's slow things down here and calm ourselves. Emotions are running high and we're both on edge and I think we're both overacting."

She clenched her fists and stomped her foot. "I'm not the one overreacting! The way you're minimizing my feelings is seriously pissing me off!"

"Calm down, Cailean. Why are you getting so excited over something so small?"

"Because instead of offering me your full support, you use the tension between me and Wilson to make judgments and criticize me and him. It's not your place. I know neither one of us is perfect, but you don't need to point it out all the time. You are so passive-aggressive and don't even realize it."

She walked out of the bedroom and heard Emerson grab his glass of wine and hurry after her.

"C'mon, Cailean, don't you think this is being blown way out of proportion?"

"The day I left Wilson's house I promised myself that I would never allow anyone to mistreat me again. I've been putting up with bad men long enough."

He mustered a soft tone. "I know and I'm sorry about that," he said, and reached to touch her arm.

She spun on her heels and smacked his hand.

"I don't want you touching me!"

He rubbed the sting the slap left behind. "Ouch."

"Keep your hands off of me."

"This is insane. I wasn't trying to criticize you," he said. "All I was trying to say is that it makes me crazy to see you getting hurt by him. I understand you've been through a lot in your life. And yes, I understand you don't want to talk about it. It's just that I think you've been through enough and maybe if you try and open up a little more, you might not get angry so quick."

"And I think you should worry about yourself a little bit more and look at what you're becoming. Show me your friends and I will show you who you are."

"What?"

"That's what my father used to say to me when I was a kid. If you stop to think about it there's a ring of truth to it, isn't there?"

Emerson stared at her, his expression soft with subtle hints of regret.
15
"You know I can't leave things like this."

"So you'd rather keep making things worse?"

"I don't like things unfinished, especially when they're messy like this."

"Just go! Get the hell out of here!"

"Why won't you let me get any closer to you?"

She fixed him with a resentful stare. "People who try and get close to me end up getting hurt."

"I care about us," Emerson said.

She tittered. "Don't start getting all soft on me. There is no us and never was."

He looked at her with disbelief. "How can you say that?"

"Say what?" Her eyes were wide with the question. "Don't you want to hear the truth?"

"If there was never an us, then what is all of this?"

He held his arms open and she stared at him and shook her head.

"What?" he said. "Why are you shaking your head at me?"

"Just look at you, Emerson, and then look at me. I think you'll be able to figure this one out without my having to spell it out. Go ahead, take a moment, I'm sure it will come to you."

His shoulders went limp and he closed his eyes. "You have got to be kidding me, Cailean."

"What am I saying that's not true?"

"Not this again."

"Yes, this again. Maybe it didn't register the last time I said it because you still think there is an us somewhere in the middle of all this drama."

He took a deep breath and opened his eyes, clearly trying to hide the hurt behind them.

"You offer me sympathy and money and that is what keeps me around," she said.

"Just listen to yourself."

"You're the one that needs to listen. Explain to me how my touching your pecker translates into my really giving a crap?" She loaded the dishes into the dishwasher and wiped down the counters. "Do you really think I would let you touch me if your wallet wasn't so full and I wasn't numb and dumb with all the beer and wine you give me?"

"Stop it, Cailean."

"It's blatantly obvious to me, and for some strange reason you choose to ignore it."

"I never thought you would go this far to try and hurt me."

"Surprise. I know how it must hurt to hear the fact that alcohol and money are my motivators, but I am telling you the truth. I'm just trying to survive."

"Are you done?" he said, his hands balled into two tight fists.

"It was your decision to stick around so now you're going to hear what I have to say. I don't care how much it hurts you either."

Silence crowded the room as she waited for him to say something else. But he just stood there red in his face and sweating like a pig.

"What are you going to do, leave me for good?" she said and raised a brow. "Stop paying the rent because you're pissed at me?" She snickered. "I doubt it."

"You're right," Emerson said, his hands relaxing at his sides. "That's because I care too much about you to do that."

"Why? Do you like being spoken to this way?"

"What I don't like is the way Wilson twists things around, and I like it even less because of the way it translates into you crapping all over me."

"What does anything I just said to you have to do with Wilson?"

He stared at her with his mouth hanging open.

"This is about you and me," she said. "It's like you're obsessed with him or something. It's really weird."

"No," he said. "That's not it at all."

"Then what is it? Because I'm trying to understand."

"This has everything to do with Wilson and the way he treats you. You're the one who has told me everything he's ever done to you. How could I not despise him? And you might not see it, but every time you hang up the phone with him, it's like you turn into this raging bull and pick a fight with me."

She waved a hand at him. "Oh, get over it, you big baby."

"Stop with the name calling. I'm trying to have an intelligent conversation with you and you're making it nearly impossible."

"Why do you think this—" she swirled her hand in the air, "—is OK?"

He stared at her again but didn't offer an explanation.

"The part that confuses me the most is that you knew what I was like getting into it," she said.

"I know," he said softly. "And I still accept it."

"I'm sure you have your reasons, Emerson. Whatever they are, I don't care."

She turned her back to him.

"I really need to get this house cleaned up before I go get Beau. You should leave," she said.

Emerson went into the living room and Cailean followed. She watched as he gathered some clothes that had been taken off throughout the house.

"It's OK, you don't need to do that," she said. "You can go, really, I'm more than capable of doing this. It'll give me some time to unwind before I get him."

"No," he said. "I helped create the mess and I will help clean it."

He loaded an armful of clothes he had collected into the washing machine.

"Maybe we should hang some pictures on the walls to make it a little more inviting for him."

"No," she said. "Regardless of what I said before, I don't want any pictures. I didn't even want that picture frame here. Look at what it did. The bare walls do me just fine. There are no painful memories for me to look at."

"I'm fine with that, if that is the way you want it."

"Of course you are," she said.

"I want to make you happy."

"Then let me do this."

"OK," he said.

"It will only be for a few days," she said. "I think the time away might do us some good."

"Before I go, I want you to know that what happened to Beau was nothing more than a freak accident. It wasn't your fault."

Cailean stared at him. "I don't think you believe that is true. Sometimes I see the way you look at me. You pity me and try to figure ways to cure me of my burdens. Stop wasting your time—I'm a lost cause."

"I don't think I'm wasting my time and I don't believe you're a lost cause either. You're a good person that's been dealt a lousy hand."

She scoffed. "I couldn't imagine what you think you are accomplishing by locking yourself in this apartment with me all day everyday and drinking constantly."

He motioned to speak but she didn't want to hear it.

"I'm a drunk, Emerson, and so are you," she said.

"We're not drunks."

"Well, if anyone knows that a drunk typically denies the fact that they are a drunk, it's me."

"I don't see anything wrong with us having a few drinks. We've been through a lot lately."

"We?" She sneered. "There you go with that again. What do you know of the pain I've experienced? What have you lost? Custody of your daughter to a woman you tried to buy?"

"I don't know why you think that."

"How else would you get her?" she said.

"Why are you so angry all the time?"

"And why are you so simpleminded? We fight when we're sober, drink at first light, and don't stop until we pass out." She leaned against the counter. "You really believe that is somehow OK?"

"I don't think we fight that often, and I don't think our drinking is that big of a deal."

"And how often did you do this before I came along?"

He pressed his lips together.

"Show me your friends, Emerson . . ."

"Do you remember us having this exact conversation only last week?"

"And we had one just like it the week before that," she said.

"Yeah, I remember that, too. You had us clean all of the alcohol out of the house and you swore you were done with it. I agreed with you, and yet that same night you got into it with Wilson. You stormed out of the house after yelling at me for allowing you to throw away all of the alcohol and you returned home with enough beer and wine to last us two weeks or better. Do you remember that? Because we opened the last of that wine this morning."

Those words stirred the feeling of panic she had when she realized she didn't have any alcohol in the house that day. She learned a valuable lesson to never do that again. It was irrational thinking and dangerous.

"And when you brought the alcohol home and I refused to drink it with you," he said, "you told me how fat and ugly I was then, too. I even remember that you told me to get out of your house and that you didn't need my money and that I made you sick."

Her gaze made its way back to Emerson. "And I told you right after we met that you couldn't fix me."

"But that's what you don't get. I don't want to fix you."

"How could you not want to?"

"All I want is to be with you. That's all I can think about."

"I broke you," she said. "I pulled you right into the quicksand with me and it has you up to your chin."

"No. I've already told you that you couldn't make me do anything I wouldn't have done myself."

She turned her back to Emerson and pressed her palms on the countertop. She looked at the walls and the shit-brown color they were. "I don't like a lot of things, Emerson. I don't like the color of these damn walls and I don't like what I've done to my son. I don't treat you well and I did the same thing to Wilson for years. My childhood was a disaster and I guess the only thing that can make me comfortable in my own skin is a drink."

She paused to gather her thoughts.

"No," she said. "I meant to say drinks—a lot of them. And knowing that?" She shook her head. "It makes me feel weak." She hid her eyes. "I dragged you into a big fat mess and you know it. Here is your out."

She stared at Emerson and gave him a moment to consider those words. The pockmarks on his cheeks were deep and distracting and they reminded her of Swiss cheese. Sweat glistened on his forehead and he breathed heavily. He was taking too long, but she swallowed the next insult.

Emerson stepped forward and Cailean's eyes widened, ready to fend him off.

"You've brought me nothing but joy," he said. "I don't like to see you hurting like this." He reached for her. "I want you to know that I love you."

She pulled away, her expression overcome by disbelief and outrage. "What did you just say to me?"

Emerson firmed up. "I told you that I love you."

She slammed her fist into the countertop. "I told you to never say those words to me!"

"Why shouldn't I say it when it's true?"

"Shut up!" she shouted, and pushed her way past him. "You've crossed the line this time and there is no going back from it." She moved to the window and pulled the shade aside. The endless snow and ice and strong gusts of wind replicated her feelings.

"I know you don't want to hear this," he said. "But I don't regret telling you that."

She turned to him and pointed a finger at him. "You see? This is what I'm talking about! You need to learn when to shut your mouth." Spit flew from her mouth and she could feel her face filling with a brilliant red. "You stupid, fat—"

"No!" he shouted back. "I'm not going to allow you to do this!"

"Get out of here!"

"I'm not going!"

"I said to gather your stuff and get out!"

Emerson pounded his chest with his fist. "I am sick and tired of this."

"You did this! We agreed to never say those words. That's not what this is."

He studied her. "Maybe you're right. Maybe you are damaged beyond repair."

She waved her hands. "Well then, what is keeping you here? Not a damn thing!"

Emerson grabbed his coat out of the closet. He checked his pocket for his wallet and keys. "You chase me away because I tell you that I love you."

"I chase you away because I don't deserve it. You will never understand. . ."

"You do, but you're unwilling to see it," he said. "I guess I don't understand the way you think and I guess I never will."

He opened the front door and the biting cold swooped through the house and Cailean backed away. She just stared at him and felt dirty and confined in her own skin.

"I guess if you want to talk to me ever again you will call me," he said, and exited the house with a shake of his head and a slam of the door.

She wiped her eyes and the stillness was instant and intense. She was lost and completely alone. Four thick walls made of self-pity and reinforced with the sins of her past held her prisoner. There were no doors to allow her passage and the walls were too tall to climb.

"Why can't you understand that I don't deserve to be loved?" she said to the closed door. She scanned the room and found the wine glass Emerson had placed on the countertop. It beckoned her.

"I don't deserve to be loved by you or anyone else," she said and hurried to the wine and carried it to the couch. She sat, turned on the digital picture frame, and watched the slideshow. She sipped the mauve liquid and struggled to think of ways to make things better.

"I need to stop drinking," she said, and meant it. She raised the glass and nodded. "I'll have this last one to help take away some of the tension, and then I'll stop."

The picture of her and Beau at the park appeared and she emptied the remainder of the wine out of the glass.

You said this was the last drink and that you would stop.

"That's not enough," she said and paid the voice inside no attention.

You had enough.

"That has to be the dumbest thing I've ever heard, so shut up," she said to the frail voice of reason still within her.

She went upstairs for the bottle of wine that was left on her nightstand. She was certain she would find a better plan hidden somewhere near the bottom of that bottle.

5

SEEING DEATH

Present day.

Cailean stood in the center of the light, oblivious to her whereabouts. Disoriented by the impossible task of trying to organize her thoughts, she had awoken from her memory with a heavy buzz from the alcohol she consumed after Emerson left her. Feeling dizzy and having a terrible stomachache, she bent over and moaned.

"Take a moment and allow it to run its course," the harsh voice from the unlit space said. "Those are merely residual feelings you've taken back with you and they will pass."

She couldn't resist the pain any longer and collapsed to a knee.

"I don't know how I used to do this to myself every day," she said, and clamped her eyes shut. The deep, gut-wrenching ache forced tears from her eyes. "I feel like hell."

"When someone is hurting they will do desperate things to try and escape the pain."

The tone of his voice and the way it penetrated her being made her body ache worse. Certainly having to argue with Wilson or fight with Emerson was so much more appealing than this. She'd even prefer to bask in her misery over Beau and what she did to him.

"I know that now," she said and dry heaved. She spit and wiped her mouth with her wet, stretched out sleeve. "I don't know all of the details yet, but I know I did something unthinkable to my son. I mistreated Wilson and used Emerson along the way and didn't care about their feelings. I know my childhood was bad, but whatever it is that happened, these big events we keep dancing around, they obviously turned me into this self-destructive, intolerable person."

The wind responded with a strong gust that nearly pushed her over. It was powerful and it reminded her of the shoves she had received from ill-intentioned kids that would surround her in grade school. They would volley her back and forth and tease her about her father, calling him a jailbird. She would argue back, stating that he was in prison and there was a big difference between the two.

"Hold on," she said, and tried to focus on the memory. "I think I just remembered something about my father. I was teased as a kid because he was in prison for some reason."

"Yes," he said. "You did many horrible things in your life. But the big event you speak of didn't define you. It only managed to exacerbate your personality flaws and push you further into addiction. Your actions have cost the people closest to you great emotional torment. You deserve nothing less."

Those words remained out there undisputed and they seeped into the wet snow at her feet. She wanted to pick them up and throw them back at him, but she couldn't. She had nothing to say.

"I can't do this anymore," she said. She wanted to drop to the floor and curl into the fetal position. Maybe she would find some respite from Sariel's reproachful gaze and his gritty, frightening voice. And most of all, she wanted to escape the scrutiny of the light and the unforgiving elements that continued to work on her fortitude.

"Oh, but you must," he said. "Even though there is only pain left for you."

"I just want to escape this madness."

"This madness is your life."

She rubbed her eyes and nodded her head in acceptance.

"It's ironic how you spent most of your life trying to forget who you were, and now, here you are, desperate for the smallest hint of your past."

Her inability to remember anything beyond what she was shown was like being an animal chained to a wall and starved for many days: She stands ready at the sound of her master's approach, tail wagging and saliva building in anticipation of the coming meal. But when the bowl of food is placed down, it is positioned just out of reach and she struggles for it. The chain is thick and strong; it pulls tightly and is unforgiving.

"Damn," she said, and wanted to scream.

The bowl of food was the answers of her past and the chain was the light that bound her. And the master?

She shuddered.

"Get a chair," he said. "I want you to position it at the edge of the light and have a seat."

Cailean did as instructed, and when she sat, something within the darkness flickered and revealed Sariel in a strange way. Black on black with a slice of dull gray between the two exposed his form in much greater detail. And what she saw was undeniably tragic and yet somehow beautiful.

Unable to comprehend what stood before her, she looked at something that resembled a man. It was constructed of dark light and was tall and thin. He had a severe hunch to his back and crooked limbs. A tremble throughout his entire body was obvious and generated a quiet rattle she hadn't noticed until now. A wheeze accompanied each labored breath, and with it, absolute peace touched her delicately and consumed her completely.

In an instant, all the burdensome wonder of who she was and what horrendous things she might have done no longer existed.

"Do you feel that?" he said.

Unable to speak a word, she nodded.

"That is what I have to offer the dead. Do you wish to know that peace?"

"Yes."

"Then tell me, what do you see standing before you?"

"The image of a man," she said and studied what she saw. "You are very tall and skinny and you're . . ."

Her bliss was torn away as quick as it came and was replaced by a profound sadness she couldn't understand.

"I'm what?" Sariel said.

She struggled to speak the words. "You're crippled."

"Your inflection suggests you're disgusted by my condition."

"No," she said, certain about it. "I'm just overwhelmed with sadness for some reason. I find it terrible that your service to the dead has caused you this."

"I have traveled an enormous, never-ending road. The daunting, interminable task that started so long ago has ravaged my body and I have grown tired."

"I'm so sorry," she said and shielded her eyes from the overhead light with her hands to try to see his face but the glare was insistent and blocked out any of the fine details.

"Why?" he said. "Why does my deformity affect you so?"

"I . . ." she fell silent and tried to identify the reason. "I'm not sure."

"I understand and I've brought you the reason."

A black box slid into the circle of light. Curiosity brought Cailean to her feet and she inspected the box with caution.

"What's inside it?" she said.

"It holds the answer to one of the many questions of what happened to Beau."

6

DYSFUNCTION

The past.

Cailean leaned against her bedroom wall and took a deep breath. The room quivered and the feeling of nausea intensified and consumed her completely. She held a bottle of wine in one hand and reached the other hand out and tried to take hold of a nearby dresser. Swaying, she fell into the dresser and swept trinkets away sending them crashing to the floor as she tried to grab onto something that would keep her upright. She managed to secure her grip on the beveled corner of the dresser.

"I've got this," she mumbled and struggled to maintain her balance.

A rolling cramp filled her stomach. Without warning the pain raced up her throat and came out as a forceful belch. Bile coated her tongue and her eyes were bright with tears.

"Damn," she said and spit on the floor. She released her grip on the dresser to wipe her mouth and fell pliant. She hit the floor hard and flopped on her side.

A maniacal laugh escaped her mouth and filled the room as she howled at how clumsy and outright drunk she was. The sound of her fitful titter mimicked that of the thing that filled her head and helped keep the pang in her soul fresh. But still, within the emptiness that was inside, there was a small part of her that desired something good. She always had a need to keep it quiet and chose to sedate it with heavy doses of alcohol and plenty of confrontation.

"Don't forget that everything is my fault," she slurred and laughed some more. "Why wouldn't it be? I'm an easy target."

To her surprise, she'd held onto the bottle of wine she had before she fell and hadn't spilled a drop.

"Look at me," she mumbled with a celebratory smile and held it up like a trophy. Laboring to get herself into a sitting position, she licked her lips. Swinging the bottle awkwardly, she brought it to her waiting lips and tilted her head back in anticipation.

She lost her balance and pitched backwards. The wine splashed her face and she slapped both hands on the ground to keep herself from falling over.

"Oh no," she said and watched in horror as the bottle rolled away from her, spilling its precious cargo with each departing turn. She gave the wet floor and the bottle a long, indignant stare as if it had cheated her somehow.

"Drunken idiot," she said, and crawled to the spilled wine. She lapped the small puddle off of the floor and picked up the bottle. Shaking it, she could hear the remaining liquid sloshing around. At least a mouthful or better remained and that encouraged her to finish it, but this time she did so with care.

When she was done, the anguish within remained unsatisfied by what she provided it and demanded something more.

You should kill yourself. No one will care and it would do a lot of people a favor.

Those words and the desire to obey them brought back a memory she would rather forget. Rolling up her sleeves, she looked at the raised scar tissue that started at the center of either wrist and sinuously extended along the entire length of her forearm. They stopped at the antecubital fossas—reminders of how low she had sunk. She avoided looking at them and often opted to wear long sleeve shirts year round.

The disfigurement twisted her expression into pure disgust. Her suffering had made her desperate—and that made her dangerous.

She looked away only to discover her reflection in a mirror that hung on the back of a closet door that had been left ajar. The person that stared back at her had an expression of untainted hate.

She looked away, familiar with and even satisfied by what she saw. The question of whether she ever really intended on dying that day or if it was merely a cry for help was answered by the voice that often called her a coward.

"But what does it matter?" she said. "What does any of it matter?"

Regardless of what she had said to Emerson about quitting drinking alcohol, she would continue to do so. It was the only way she could repress the sorrow. And that voice that tried to guide her—it wasn't nice and yet she couldn't ignore it.

She crawled back to the dresser and used it to pull herself to her feet.

Tell me when it becomes about Beau first in your decision making?

Wilson's question resonated in her head like a penny that bounced around inside of a tin can.

"Shut up," she said.

When, Cailean?

"Oh, Beau," she said. "What kind of mother treats her child the way I have treated you?"

She pushed back against the idea of ever having to hear the response to that question.

"No," she said and held a hand up. "Please, don't answer that. I don't think I could bear ever hearing you tell me what you really think of me. I know I'm a lousy mother, but to actually hear you say it?" She shook her head. "That would be devastating."

She released her hold on the dresser and stumbled to the bed and fell face down. Emerson's scent trapped within the linens was powerful and the desire to have him near stirred in her groin.

Amused, she chuckled at how often she was repulsed by him and yet desired him when he wasn't around.

Just like the bottle.

He was one of the few that were willing to put up with her crap and she couldn't figure out why.

"Because you're a big fat stupid man that thinks you can get away with telling me you love me."

She sighed and was overtaken by a sudden burst of anger.

"Damn you, Emerson!"

She slapped the bed and tossed a pillow across the room.

"Why would you stand by my side, especially when you know what I did?"

And then she remembered how he helped her cover it up.

"Because you're a lot like me, aren't you?"

She nodded, certain the memory was true.

"Maybe I should have stayed with Wilson. He understood me the most. I couldn't understand him because he was ordinary."

But he didn't want you.

"Shut up," she said and attempted to relax and concentrate on the numbness that consumed her. She offered it her hand and allowed it to lead her far away from her concerns. And there, tethered to an artificial euphoria, the nudge of sleep came quickly and made her body twitch as it pulled her farther away.

"Wilson," she said half awake.

There was no doubt that he was in love with her and had always treated her well. He treated her much better than she deserved despite the fact she offered nothing but a bag full of dysfunctions and lies in return. His ability to forgive and to see the good in her made her resent him. So she made up a bunch of lies about him and told them to Emerson. How else could she make sure they were at odds with each other so they wouldn't look into her stories?

Brilliant.

And although the love she had for Wilson was there, it was buried deep beneath a pile of perverse thinking and cruel motivations, never to be disclosed.

"Maybe if you supported me the way you should have when I needed you most instead of . . ." she snickered. "Ah, it's like I said, what does it matter? What's done is done and I can't change it."

And, like someone flipping a switch, she fell asleep and was immediately drawn into the memory of that day.

7

TOO LATE

The past.

Cailean pushed the heavy blanket aside and placed her hand on the floor. She used this tactic often after a night of binge drinking to help keep the room from spinning and reduce the nausea.

"It's after two o'clock," he said. She felt too lousy to care that Wilson had come to lecture her again and didn't think she could lift her head to give him a dirty look even if she tried.

"Cailean, did you hear what I said?"

He sat at the bottom of the couch by her feet and he tapped his foot aggressively. He always did that when he was upset.

"Please stop shaking the couch," she said.

"Then answer me when I ask you something."

"Just keep your voice down and stop shaking the couch, OK?"

"I don't like it when you don't answer me," he said.

"I know, Wilson. I'm exhausted and you just woke me up, what do you expect?"

"It's two pm."

The windows were covered with heavy curtains and she had hung clothing off the curtain rod to block out any daylight that might enter the room through the slightest crack.

"I don't care what time it is," she said. "Leave me alone and let me get back to sleep. I'm tired."

"You're not tired, you're hung over again. There's a big difference."

"What's it to you anyway?"

"It is everything to me, Cailean."

A persistent ache in the back of her head was accompanied by a full body tremble that begged for more alcohol.

"You're totally creeping me out," she said. "How long have you been sitting there watching me?"

"Long enough to know that as bad as I'm going to feel about it, I know this is the right thing for me to do."

"What are you talking about? You're not even making any sense." Her face was pressed into the cushion and her hand remained firmly on the floor. "Why don't you just go away and leave me alone?"

He pulled the blanket off of her completely and she looked at him with intense irritation.

He lifted a bottle of Jack Daniels out of his lap and waited until she looked at it. He turned it upside down and not a single drop came out.

"You are a drunk," he said, and dropped the empty bottle on the floor. The loud clunk made her sit up.

"What is wrong with you?" she said.

"Look at what you've done to Beau's playroom," he said. His eyes were locked somewhere in the distance, focused on his agenda. "You've turned it into this dark chamber of self-pity. I feel depressed just coming in here."

"Why don't you lower your voice, Wilson? You know damn well that I'm not feeling well."

"I am done giving you free passes. You continue to do this to yourself day after day and there is nothing I can do to help you anymore."

"How did I ever guess?" she said. "As soon as I woke up and realized it was you sitting there, I knew that this would turn into a lecture session. Spare me, would you?" She settled on her side, muscled the blanket away from Wilson, and pulled it over her head.

"I didn't come here to lecture you. That hasn't changed a thing, and if I'm going to be honest with myself, I don't think anything I say or do ever will. I've come here to tell you that your behavior is unacceptable and it will not be tolerated anymore. Beau is at my mom's house and he will remain there until tomorrow. I'm giving you until then to be out of the house."

She pulled the blanket down, stared at him for a second, and then laughed.

"You can't kick me out of the house. It's as much mine as it yours."

"No, not anymore. You will go because I'm not going to give you any other choice."

She sat up again and the nausea followed her. She realized that her wild hair, probably reaching out in all directions, and her puffy eyes and tired face contorted into a look of disbelief made her look even more deranged. "You know, why don't you cut the crap? This isn't funny and I get the message. Let's wait until I'm feeling a little better so we can talk about it rationally."

Wilson shook his head. "What annoys me most about this entire thing is that you weren't considerate enough not to get yourself drunk because of the appointment."

"What appointment?"

He heaved a sigh. "Beau had an appointment at the doctor's office today and you made a promise to him that you would come."

She swung her feet onto the floor. "I'll get dressed! How long until we have to be there?"

He shook his head again, this time for a while. "You are so lost inside that bottle. It's like you haven't heard a thing I've said to you."

She stared at him blankly, her mind inconceivably disorganized.

He stood, walked to the curtains, and yanked them down. Light flooded the room and Cailean clamped her eyes shut and turned her head.

"What are you doing?"

"I've already told you that the morning has come and gone," he said. "Beau has already been to the doctor's and he is now at my parents' house so he doesn't have to see this."

"See what? Why didn't you wake me?"

"I tried, but you wouldn't budge."

She shook her head and shoved the blanket onto the floor. "You didn't try and wake me! You did this on purpose so you could use it as an excuse to get me out of the house."

She stood, teetered, and sat again.

"Look at you," Wilson said, his voice full of pity. "You can't even stand up."

"I can stand just fine. I just woke up out of a deep sleep and I need a few more minutes to gather myself."

"Beau cried because he couldn't understand why you weren't there."

She clamped her eyes shut. "Why do you always have to tell me this?"

"Because it is the truth. That is what you do to him. He thinks the reason you didn't go was because of his condition. He asked me if you were embarrassed by it."

"Of course I'm not embarrassed. You told him that, right?" she said, her eyes as wild as her hair.

"I wouldn't tell him anything bad about you. I'm not going to do that. But you need to know that you are making an impression on him that is going to last a lifetime. It is going to set a tone about the way he feels about himself and the way he interacts with others."

"I know what I've done. I don't need you to keep reminding me."

"Maybe I don't because it doesn't seem to make a bit of difference. He's only eight years old and he's been through more crap than most fifty-year-olds. Why can't you just stop and be normal for his sake?"

"How am I supposed to answer that? There's no switch I can flip. It's just not that easy."

"I don't know, Cailean. I guess I want to know what is going on inside of you and how I can help you deal with it."

"You can't."

"And that's it?"

"I resent you for always making it my fault. I've never heard you once accept any responsibility in this."

"You're right," he said and bobbed his head. "I am to blame for allowing this to go on for as long as it has." He picked up the bottle of Jack Daniels and set it down on the end table. He walked out of the room. "I can't believe what you have become," he said as he walked down the hall. "Just make sure you are out of the house by morning."

She inspected the room she was in and saw what Wilson was talking about: she had barricaded herself in and the light exposed her filth. Separated from her family and the rest of the world, she caged herself in with the nasty thing that lived inside of her.

"Oh, here," Wilson said, returning to the room. He removed an envelope from his pocket and leaned it against the empty whiskey bottle. "There is enough money in there for a hotel room and some food for a few days. I suggest you don't drink it away. Maybe you can call your boyfriend to help you out. I don't know if he's any better than you and I don't really care anymore. I just hope you are sober enough to know that

44

there are no more chances and that I have never been so serious about something as I am about this."

"Wilson?"

"I don't care what you take or intend to destroy because you're pissed at me so as long as it doesn't belong to Beau. Like I said, I will be back with him in the morning, and for your sake, you better be long gone by then."

"Wilson!"

"I don't want to get the police or Child Protective Services involved, but I will call them if I have to."

"Please, don't do this to me."

"I'm not doing anything to you. You did this all by yourself."

"I'll stop drinking and go back to seeing my doctor. If I miss an appointment, then you can tell me to leave. Give me a chance to fix this. Please, I don't want you to give up on me. Not now."

He shook his head.

"We're way past that now. You won't stop until you realize how big of a problem you really have."

"You're doing this because you blame me for what happened to Beau."

"What I blame you for is being a drunk."

"Look at what happened to me as a kid! How can you think that is easy to live with?"

"I know it hasn't been easy. But when we married and decided to have a child you said that was behind you. We agreed on therapy and counseling, but after a while you decided that you didn't want to do that. I don't know what happened or where we went wrong, but you started drinking again and it quickly grew into this."

"I never stopped drinking, Wilson. It is the only thing that eases the pain and stifles the memories."

"Like I said, shame on me for not seeing it sooner and for allowing it to get this far. I don't know, maybe you should have focused your energy on mothering your son. If you did that instead of floundering in your misery I'm sure it would have helped lessen your pain."

"Oh, Wilson, please."

"You chose to drink and neglect your family. The worst part is you're screwing up your own kid because of some awful man that lived across the street from you when you were a child. I figured you would have learned from that, knowing how a dysfunctional adult could affect a child as it did you."

"You don't know how awful it was."

"Then why wouldn't you learn from that and try and protect our son from it?"

Her face reddened.

"Just go and get the hell outta here!" she waved a dismissive hand, stood, and pushed her way past him. She walked to the kitchen and yanked open the refrigerator. She took out a beer.

"There is nothing you can say to me that I haven't thought of already."

"You need to stop drinking," he said.

"Don't tell me what to do."

She opened the beer and drank.

"I told you that you cannot do this here anymore!" He snatched the beer out of her hand. She reached for it, but he pulled it away.

"Do you know how hard it is living with the memory of what was done to me and what I did to you and Beau? Can't you try and grasp for one second what it must be like for me?"

He dumped the beer into the sink.

"Yes, Cailean, I can because we've been living it with you every single day. It's what you are, it's a part of your anatomy, and I cannot accept that any longer."

She got another beer.

"Look at you," he said. "You're drunk all the time and you disappear for days. Your husband and son shouldn't have to wonder where you are and whether or not you're ever going to come home again."

Tears rolled down her cheeks. "You say you know what it is like, that you've had to live it with me, but I can assure you that you don't know what it is like. You couldn't possibly know what it feels like in here." She pounded her chest.

"Please, stop feeling sorry for yourself all the time, Cailean. It is pitiful and it has worn me out."

He grabbed the beer out of her hand, cracked it open, poured it out, and crushed the can.

"I can never escape the thought of what I have done to him or my father," she said, her eyes filled with a mix of regret and frustration.

"You didn't do anything to your father. He did what he did to protect you." He walked to the front door and paused. "And you've let his sacrifice stand for nothing."

"How can you be so cruel?" she shouted and cried harder. "I don't know where you expect me to go from here. I really don't."

"Now you will have plenty of time to figure that out."

He looked at her over his shoulder.

"And don't bother trying to find all of your stashes of beer, wine, and booze throughout the house. They are all gone. I got rid of them before I woke you. I left those last few beers in the refrigerator to see how much we really meant to you. I am certain I understand now."

He exited the house and gently closed the door.

For the first time in a very long time, Cailean was sober. The sudden realization that she had been forsaken stifled her buzz and brought her back to reality. The pain in this moment was more intense than the memory of her past. She collapsed to the floor and submitted herself to a steady flow of tears.

8

TRUMPET LILIES

Present day.

"Cailean?" Sariel said.

The untamed sound of his voice startled her. She had been focused on the ebony wall and how it succeeded in containing her. Merely an expanse absent of light, it filled her with such angst and did so without words.

"What are you thinking?" he said.

"About the obscurity and how it troubles me. And that box," she said, and looked at it by her feet. "There's something about it that I don't like at all." She backed away from it.

"Why do you think it troubles you so?"

"I know there's something inside it that I don't want to see."

"But you know you must," he said.

She nodded. "I know."

"Look straight ahead. Try to focus on me."

The gray light that surrounded him remained unabated and she watched him with a steady focus, not knowing what to expect.

"Forget about the box by your feet and let us talk about your glimpse into the past," he said. "What did you get out of everything you saw?"

She turned to her thoughts and didn't like what she felt. "That I was unloved and rejected when I was at my lowest."

"But you were nothing more than a virus."

"I was a product of my environment."

"So what was Wilson to do with you?"

"He should have helped me."

"He tried so many times, but you refused to listen. Should he have allowed you to continue to disrupt the household and contaminate his son?"

"You are talking as if I were some kind of incurable disease."

"I told you that you were a virus."

Cailean scrunched her brows. "Beau was my child, too."

"Yes, he was. Maybe you should have recognized it then."

Those words dug deep but she refused to show it.

"I tried, but Wilson wouldn't let me."

"Oh yes, he did. Maybe he shouldn't have let you, but he did."

"He took everything away from me. He told me to leave. I was discarded like a piece of trash."

Sariel remained in the same spot he had been in before she descended into her memory. His skinny, crooked legs appeared as if they would break underneath his large upper body. His gnarled hands and long, wiry fingernails hung by his side like the tangle of a small bush.

"Yes, you were told to go and deservingly so."

"I was hurting and needed support and understanding—not the cold shoulder. I don't know. There is a part of me that wished Wilson would have told me everything that happened to our marriage and Beau was my fault."

"Even though it was, you know he never would have done that."

"I know he wouldn't and you couldn't imagine how annoying that was. Maybe if he did, maybe it would have made things easier."

"For whom?"

"For me!" She threw her hands up and shook her head in disgust. "Having the world hate me in return might have justified the way I felt inside."

"You know that his verbal charge would have done nothing for you. The way you were is the way you have been since you were a child. You thrive off of negativity and you are cunning, devious, and manipulative. Search within and you might catch a glimpse."

She didn't want to look for it. She wanted to leave it alone and get as far away from it as she could.

"I could never imagine that death would be like this," she said. "Being locked inside of a prison constructed of light and dark, forced to face the terrible choices of my life in interrupted sequences. It is infuriating."

"You are yet to reach your breaking point, Cailean. But I assure you, it will come."

"And you are a bastard like the rest of them!"

She watched the smear of gray with wide, expecting eyes. Ready for his penalizing words or even physical contact, she waited. But instead, he bent down and picked up the thing that was the stain on the black and lifted it over his head. And in an instant, Sariel's light was gone.

"No, don't leave me," she said, and became desperate. "That's what my father, Wilson, Beau, and Emerson did to me. Please, not you, too. I didn't mean what I said."

An overpowering aroma of flowers filled Cailean's nose and visions of trumpet lilies—pink, white, yellow, and orange—occupied her head. Suddenly, she was a young girl at the age of nine. She ran through a field with her arms outstretched, holding firmly onto something unknown in either hand, and she batted the four-foot tall flower stems with focused anger and private joy.

"Cailean!"

The sound of the angry man's voice frightened her. It had come from behind and she ducked down to elude it. She discarded the things she was holding in the thicket off to the right and crawled on the ground for several feet. She turned left into the heavy foliage and quickly settled. The sound of her own pounding heart and heavy breathing brought her hands to her mouth to try to stifle the gasps.

"Cailean?"

The sudden nearness of heavy footsteps filled her with a growing fear and she regretted her decision to hide.

"You know I'm going to find you sooner or later so you might as well come out now and save me the trouble," he said. "Things are too thick down there so you won't get very far. Now, I'm going to give you to the count of three to come out on your own and face me."

Mr. Hagen was a mean old man who drove an old truck and grunted at everyone around him.

"One," he said.

She hadn't noticed the rust bucket in the driveway when she decided to trespass and execute her crazy idea.

"Two."

He farmed like her father did, but he always did it better. The product her father put out was inferior to Mr. Hagen's. They grew half as tall and never popped with color like his did. This had somehow created hardships for her family that she didn't fully comprehend, but she had an idea on how she could fix it.

"Last chance."

Maybe he was bluffing and would give up his search, thinking she was long gone.

"Three."

Mr. Hagen dropped to his knees and grinned at her. "Get over here," he said and reached for her. He grabbed her ankles.

She screamed and kicked and tried to back away, but the brush was too thick and held her in place. Something touched her feet and she looked at the black box that teetered on the tips of her shoes. She was back beneath the circle of light with Sariel lurking somewhere close.

"Those lilies," she said. "And that man! I want to know what that was about!"

"The box at your feet. I want you to pick it up and place it on the table beneath the light," he said.

She looked at the box but ignored it. "I want to know what I was doing there and why he was after me!"

"Pick up the box and place it on the table."

She kicked the box away.

"No! I said I want to know what that was about. I'm tired of doing things your way all the time. I'm not your toy and I deserve some answers!"

Flung high into the air, Cailean hit the canopy and it had no give. Plunging to the floor face first, an unseen force pressed down on her with tremendous pressure and rendered her immobile. The oxygen was slowly being forced from her lungs and her body sunk into the ground.

The slush filled her open mouth and she tried to scream out in pain but could only manage a gurgle. Desperate for air, the thick liquid forced its way down her throat and she gasped. She flailed and clawed with every ounce of strength she had, but soon submitted to the might of her attacker.

"Do as you are instructed," he said. "This is your last chance to follow my direction or I will send you away to experience this for an eternity. Imagine what it will be like for you to always desire a breath and to never get it while constantly being tormented about the missing details of your miserable life."

She tried to respond but gurgled again. In an instant the pressure was relieved and the ground released her. She sat up and choked, belched, and vomited what filled her throat. Sucking in a painful lungful of oxygen she was dazed.

"Take the box to the table," he said.

She struggled to stand, unsure if she was hurt. When she picked up the box she found that it was light and it slipped out of her wet hands. The tingling sensation had overtaken both arms now and had begun its slow climb into her feet and the back of her calves. When she bent to retrieve the box, she lifted her pant leg and saw the white that had moved up her arms had also begun to bleach the skin on her legs.

"Your health is quickly deteriorating on the other side and your time is running short here."

She readjusted her clothes.

"I suggest you move faster," he said.

She obeyed with a subtle nod and hurried to place the box on the table.

"You wouldn't believe the things people have confessed to me," he said. "Some beg for a moment of their life back to try and complete the things they feel have been left undone. Others are happy to see me and express their appreciation for relieving their pain. And most of the people are truly angry, lost souls with no chance at redemption. But you?"

She held her chin up and kept her focus on the sound of his voice.

"You needed me so badly, and as badly as I wanted you, I just couldn't take you. It was not yet your time. The sadness in your eyes has stayed with me for so long and I have thought about you often . . ."

The rattle and the wheeze drew near and surrounded her completely.

"Come closer," he said. "Step to the edge so I can have a better look at you."

She walked straight ahead and looked at the black smear. The way it moved and swirled played tricks on her eyes and she looked at her feet to escape the confusion. She rubbed her eyes with balled fists and wanted to cry about so many things.

An extended finger with a long, knotty fingernail pierced the bright and settled underneath her chin. With the split tip of the nail coming to rest on her chin, he encouraged her focus up. And when she lifted her gaze, his wrinkled, hairless face with a displeased grimace descended upon her. His fleshy earlobes dangled past his chin and his bleached, blank eyes were impossible to understand. White cracked lips parted ever so slightly as he spoke.

"Oh yes," he said, his teeth were discolored and broken and his breath was like a waft of stale air that escaped a sealed tomb. "It is still there and hidden deep, I can see it. It doesn't want to come out, but it will, and it knows it has to. It has made you hollow and it is a big part of the reason why you are here."

Paralyzed by his touch, all she could do was listen and watch.

"Do not fear what you see looking at you right now, because what dwells within you is surely uglier than I."

Sariel curled his finger into his hand and pulled it into the shadow. He shook his head and withdrew his face. A sudden prevailing push of air howled ominously.

Cailean stumbled backwards and felt the sting his touch had left behind. She rubbed her chin. The feeling turned to a burn and started a slow crawl up her face. It moved past her lips and into her cheeks and nose.

"What did you do to me?"

It began to snow again, violently.

She continued to swipe at the sensation that now moved around her eyes and traced her hairline. Her fingers tried to brush away the feeling but her touch discovered a lump on the center of her forehead.

"What is this? Did this happen when you pushed me to the ground?"

She explored the sensitive, swollen area. Long and thin, it stretched almost the entire length of her forehead.

"You arrived here with that," he said. "I am merely making obvious what you need to know next."

She wondered how she could continue on with this insanity.

"I want you to stop toying with me!" she said, and lashed out against the darkness, intending to reach into the black and pull Sariel into the light. But it bit back like the jolt from an electrical outlet and it sent her down to the floor. She hit the back of her head, and the explosive pain invited the darkness inside her mind.

9

MAKING AMENDS

The past.

Cailean's eyelids felt like lead weights. She gagged hard and tried to combat the dizziness. The room she occupied was dark and silent and she didn't know what had awoken her.

She sat up fast, retched, and the taste of cheap wine and stomach acids filled her mouth. She swallowed it and made a face of displeasure. The time of day remained unannounced by a blinking digital clock on the nightstand.

The constant pulse of pain that occupied the inside of her head grew stronger with her emerging awareness, and her limbs trembled in response. She carefully positioned herself on the edge of the bed, placed her feet on the floor, and grabbed the sheets on either side of her hips. The room continued to undulate.

A deep, rolling pain that started in the pit of her stomach and crawled up her esophagus carried wine and undigested food. It flew out of her mouth with a violent heave. The thick, brown liquid and small chunks of solids splashed on the floor between her feet and splattered the nightstand, bed skirt, walls, and the pillow she had tossed off of the bed before she passed out. The strong, overpowering stench of stomach acids forced her to pinch her nose and breathe out of her mouth. Her belly wrenched with a second wave of pain and she vomited again.

She wiped her mouth and stood. "Beau," she said and teetered as she navigated around the mess on the floor. Using the walls and furniture to guide herself out of the bedroom, she sat down on the top step before she started downstairs. She descended on her backside.

When she reached the landing, she clamped her eyes shut, fought the urge to vomit again, and squeezed her quivering hands into tight fists.

Drawing a deep breath, she took another moment to assess the remaining distance between herself and the blinking answering machine on the end table next to the couch.

"Damn it," she said. The twenty or so steps to the machine seemed like an impossible mile.

The shade she had flicked aside earlier in the day had gotten hung up on the back of the couch. The dull light that shined through made her believe it was around dinnertime or maybe a little bit later.

Winded, she stood over the answering machine and steadied her finger enough to press the playback button.

"Mom, are you there?"

Pause.

"It's Beau. I'm waiting for you and I can't wait to see you. I love you. Bye."

The machine beeped; end of message. Her hangover was joined with severe regret and extreme guilt.

"Cailean, I told him you would call him back like you said you would and he's waiting for you. I hope you're on the way and that you don't let him down again. I really do."

The machine beeped again.

"Where the hell are you? He's been waiting all day for you. This isn't fair to him. You're selfish and could give a crap how badly you hurt him. You are unbelievable, do you know that?"

The machine gave a long, final beep that signaled the end of the messages. She tightened her lips and pressed her tongue into her teeth. She erased the messages and picked the phone up off of the couch and began to run through her catalog of excuses.

She cleared her throat, made her way into the kitchen, and opened the refrigerator. She needed to rid her mouth of the taste of vomit and grabbed a beer out of the door and cracked it open and finished it in one long gulp.

She dialed home and sighed at her thoughts. No matter how she tried to twist it, this was her fault. Maybe it was time for the truth. And maybe Wilson would be more understanding and appreciative of her new approach.

"Hello?" Wilson said, and sounded like he had just awoken.

"Wilson, it's Cailean."

"Cailean . . . why are you calling here so late?"

"I want to speak to Beau."

"It's eleven o'clock and he's sleeping."

Cailean looked at the window where the shade was hung up and realized that the streetlight made it appear as though it were dusk, not late at night. All sense of time escaped her.

The clock on the stove blinked.

"I think I lost the power or something. The storm probably pulled down some power lines. All of my clocks are blinking," she said, and made no attempt to hide her own disappointment.

Silence often gave way to the awful moment when she had to contend with the voice of reason and she didn't want to hear it.

"Did you hang up? Are you still there?" she said.

"Yes, I'm here."

"You sound mad. I'm sorry."

"I'm past being mad at you, Cailean."

She could understand that. Her word meant nothing.

Having a streetlight in front of her house after she had awoken from binge drinking had proven to be troublesome on more than one occasion.

"The streetlight in front of my place is really bright," she said and didn't mean to say it out loud. She really wanted another drink so she would have something in her mouth and she wouldn't be able to say anything stupid.

"You were drinking again like I suspected. I can hear it in your speech."

"No, I wasn't drinking when I spoke to you this morning. I didn't start until after we hung up the phone. I fell asleep and just woke up."

"I know you probably passed out. You drink until you can't stand, and yet again I'm telling you the worst part about it is that you couldn't stay away from the bottle for one day."

"I tried," she said and got another beer. It would continue to help calm her nerves and offset the headache. She drank eagerly. "I decided I would be completely honest in this phone call with you—you deserve it. I feel bad enough that I don't need you compounding it with accusations."

"I appreciate you wanting to tell the truth, I really do. But why do you always get the guilty conscience afterwards and never before?"

"I don't know, but I would like to start changing that. Emerson and I got into this really big argument this morning after you and I hung up the phone."

"I stopped caring about what happens between you and Emerson a long time ago." He breathed into the phone, his anger tangible. "You two deserve each other. What I care about is Beau and you've hurt him again."

"I know I did and I'm sorry."

"You don't owe me the apology. I've actually come to expect this from you. But I suppose there is still a side of me that hopes you find peace and it allows you to heal. I cannot believe the damage that man did to you as a child. I'm sorry you were molested, Cailean, and that he broke apart your family. I hope that man got what he deserved when he met his maker."

"Thank you, Wilson, I needed to hear that, to know you still cared," she said and began to cry.

"I just wish you never brought him with you into our home," he said.

"Yeah, me too," she said and had to shake the menacing image of Mr. Hagen from her mind's eye. "But I think what happened that day is something I will forever struggle to escape. I want you to know that I intended on coming to see Beau, but Emerson insisted that he come with me. I didn't want him to and it turned into this whole big thing."

"And it was so bad you needed to dive headlong into another bottle? Do you think your son really cares about that?"

The beer that settled in her belly felt good, but she needed more to reverse the effects of the hangover. She took another beer out of the refrigerator.

"I know it," she said. "I'm not dumb."

"No, you're not. And that is what I don't understand about you."

She popped open the can and drowned her desire to tell him off. This honesty approach opened her up and now, she realized, she was becoming his punching bag. "I'm going to stop by in the morning to see him," she said.

"I would prefer you didn't. You've done enough."

"I'm going to."

"Please don't, I'm not kidding."

"Neither am I. My mind is made up. I'm coming."

"Yeah, sure, whatever. And I wouldn't think about telling him that you were planning on stopping by because you would only disappoint him again. The sad thing though is that I feel like it is really me that's doing it to him because I'm the one that keeps telling him that you're coming."

"I don't want you to tell him," she said. "I want this to be a surprise."

"I said I don't want you here. You can't be trusted," he said.

No amount of beer could take away the pain of that truth. But she didn't see the reason for him saying it.

"This is why we can never get along, Wilson. You never give me a break."

"I can't. I'm trying to protect him from the person that keeps hurting him."

She ran stiff fingers through her hair. "No, it's because you accuse and judge me all the time and it doesn't help. There are ways for you to protect him without being so callous towards me."

A great silence wedged itself between them. "I can't emphasize it enough. I don't want you coming here," Wilson said. "I want you to understand that I have never accused you of anything you haven't done. I have sympathy for what you went through, but that was a long time ago and you chose to drag that around with you and you've allowed it to hurt us."

Cailean remembered that she wanted to speak in truth with Wilson. She wanted to tell him what really happened that day in the lily field. If she did, that might lift a tremendous burden off of her shoulders. But that truth would forever remain a secret—no matter how badly it ate her up inside or destroyed everyone around her.

"I'm sorry, Wilson, I really need to hang up now," she said. "I am going to come by tomorrow whether you like it or not."

She disconnected the call.

10

STABBING PAIN

The past.

Sariel stood close to Cailean and watched her with unwavering interest. She had been kneeling on the kitchen floor for the past half hour, swigging from a cheap gallon of vodka that now rested at her side.

"I am worthless," she muttered. "I don't even see the point in trying to continue on."

Although the words were garbled and hard to decipher, he understood them perfectly. Long ago, when this woman was just a girl, a man that was suffering terribly and needed his help in moving on brought him to her. He had spotted Cailean from a distance and was compelled to see up close what had made him so curious. What he discovered confounded him.

Often he would return to her and continue his study to try to discover what had been afflicting her. The idea that she had been born soulless weighed heavily on him, but after careful inspection, he could see traces of it within her physical form. It was trapped and wanted out of her body in the worst way.

And now as he stood before her, he watched the same struggle continue on.

She grumbled some other words, but they were slurred and indecipherable. She swayed and stumbled and Sariel moved out of her way, careful not to make contact.

She used the kitchen counter to hold herself upright and she stared at the clock.

Wilson had gone to the hospital to bring Beau home. It had been several months since the accident, and over the past several weeks he had made great progress.

"I can't face him," she said. "How can I ever look him in the eyes when I know what I did to him? I can't live with that."

She shimmied along the counter until she reached the knife rack. Selecting the biggest knife out of the holder, she tried to focus her eyes on her reflection in the stainless steel refrigerator. It was blurry and messy like her entire life.

"Worthless," she snickered.

With a steady calm, she stood upright, put the knife into her wrist, and dragged it up her forearm, zigzagging the blade as she worked it all the way to the bend in her arm. The massive cut left a gaping slit that gushed blood. She staggered around the kitchen and watched the blood spill out onto the floor.

"Look at all the blood," she said, amazed.

Switching the knife into her other hand, she struggled to hold it. The ligaments in the hacked forearm weakened her grasp tremendously and she managed a much shallower cut in the other arm that started at her wrist and also stopped at the bend in her arm before the knife slipped out of her hand and clattered across the floor.

She looked at the knife, angry that the job remained incomplete.

Exposed meat and hewed tendons pushed their way through the jagged gashes.

"I guess it will have to do," she said and shrugged. She began to dance and spin around and swing her arms aggressively. The blood flew in strands all around the kitchen. Droplets dotted across the floors, cabinets, and ceiling and she was like a painter fixated on her canvas, desperate to finish the picture. She slipped on the slick floor and landed on her back. She hit her head hard and stared at the ceiling. Open-mouthed and dizzy, she moaned in both satisfaction and pain.

Sariel stepped forward and looked down on her. Her breathing was shallow and she was already slipping in and out of consciousness.

"I am near," he said. "I know you can't see me, but you can hear me now. You long for my touch, but I won't give it to you yet. You are not meant to die this day, but soon you will. And when you do, you will wish you remained here in your misery."

He sat down next to her and studied her some more. To his surprise he glimpsed what had eluded him for so long. It was ugly and territorial and it made him apprehensive to be so near.

"You must leave her when it is my time to take her," he said and lifted his chin and listened. The sound of someone approaching the home made him stand and watch. Wilson entered the house through the front door.

"Just in time," Sariel said and was pleased he would be leaving soon. He wanted to be as far away from that thing as he could.

He watched Wilson and how he looked at Cailean as he tried to figure out what he was seeing.

"Oh my God!" Wilson said, and ran to her side. Rendered motionless by what he saw, Wilson stared. Sariel could hear his thoughts that were filled with disbelief.

"Move it," Sariel said, and clapped his hands. "You don't have time."

Wilson sprung into action. He picked up the phone and called emergency services.

"Nine one one, what's your emergency?"

Sariel could hear the words of the operator as if the person were in the room with them. "Please, send an ambulance! There's blood all over the place and my wife is on the floor. I don't think she's breathing!"

"I've dispatched the ambulance, sir. Don't hang up the phone. Are you sure she's not breathing?"

"Yes. I don't know, I can't tell. Just send an ambulance!"

"They're on their way," the operator said with a constant calm to her voice. "I need you to find out where the blood is coming from."

"I think her wrists. I can't tell . . . there's so much of it. I see a knife on the floor."

"I need you to get a towel and apply pressure to the wounds," the operator said.

Wilson dropped the phone and Sariel watched him run around in a panic. Wilson gathered towels and wrapped her wounds. He pressed down on them and whimpered.

"Stay with me, Cailean," Wilson said. "Help is on the way."

He wiped his eyes, painting his face with her blood.

"Beau is still in the hospital and he's going to be there a few more days," he said. "They're concerned about some swelling that formed around his spine. I need you here to help me through this. How could you do such a thing?"

Sariel circled them and Cailean's tortured soul reached out to him. He backed away and shook his head.

"I cannot help you yet, Cailean. But soon I will come. And when I do, I will offer you a chance to escape the madness that is your life."

11

CREEPING DEATH

Present day.

"Was I molested by the old man that was chasing me in the field?" Cailean said, and her eyes grew wide with the question. "Is he the reason why I was so dysfunctional?"

The reply Sariel gave her was silence. It had become inappropriate and it had lost its effectiveness. He showed her these things and yet wouldn't elaborate when she found herself closing in on the answers.

The unmistakable hiss of his labored breathing kept a slow, deep rhythm and she knew he was listening, waiting for her to give up on her inquiry.

"I did mean what I said to you before. You are the bastard I suspected you to be," she said.

Sariel didn't reply to her provocation and the ongoing quiet made her restless. It had instantly reverted back to being worse than anything he could say or do to her.

"That's OK," she said, and tried to hide what she felt. "You don't have to tell me because I already know. I could see the look in his eyes when he grabbed my ankles. He's a damn pervert and I was afraid of him because I knew what he was capable of doing. Right now I can feel the touch of his cold, pruned hands on my skin and it's making me sick."

She licked her lips and shivered. Something inside her stirred her emotions.

"I can feel the fear rising within me," she said. "It's like the old man is out there with you, occupying the dark. Is he watching me? Did you bring him here?"

"What if I did?" Sariel said. "What would you say to him?"

"I want him to know that I hate him and that he ruined my life. That I've been unable to love anyone other than a bottle of alcohol because of the pain he's caused me. It has been so great and I became desperate to escape it. But I learned that no matter how many times I emptied the bottle, the memory of what he did always remained."

"Good," Sariel said. "Your anger is tangible and that means it is still in you."

"Did he hear what I said? Tell him he's a son of a bitch!"

"I cannot tell him because he's not here."

She furrowed her brows and tried to comprehend his words. "What do you mean he's not here?"

"He's gone to the other side," Sariel said. "He died a long time ago."

Her shoulders went limp. "How can that be? What was I feeling?"

"Your hate and the way it controls you."

She fell to her knees and tried to cope with the idea that she was no closer to knowing who she was. The hand she had used to try to penetrate the blackness and grab Sariel throbbed without remission. She knew it was a distraction.

"You constantly try and provoke me," she said. "You stir my emotions and keep me inches away from the truth."

"The truth is in front of you."

"No, it isn't." She shook her head. "I know you made me angry on purpose. You did it to bait me into touching the darkness so you could introduce that flashback to me. I don't understand your methods and why you continue to tease me."

She grimaced.

"Why did you bring me back with such physical and mental pain?"

"Pain is a motivator. I've learned quickly it is what makes you pay attention."

She flexed her hand and shook it.

"I know the barrier you have constructed around you is strong and difficult to penetrate. The best way for me to dismantle it is to do it piece by piece. Your physical pain is there to help you understand the dangers of your being outside of the light. I took you from your body prematurely to bring you here. It was the only way I could ensure that we would have enough time to review your past. In order to make this happen, I had to provide you with shelter from the harshness of what is beyond the ability of your physical body. That is what the protection of the light you stand in provides for you."

"The only thing you have shown me is that a sick man ruined my life and that I took it out on my family. Then you toy with my emotions to simply get a rise out of me and you somehow expect this to motivate me."

"I don't regret the methods I have had to resort to in order to bring your emotions to the surface. You were a cold person that was hard to love."

Those words were powerful enough to move her into silent contemplation.

"You were even harder to like," he said.

"Will anyone mourn me at my funeral?" she asked.

"Would you?"

Everything she learned about herself filled her with certain doubt. The question of whether or not she would attend Mr. Hagen's funeral crossed her mind. The idea that she would use him as a comparison made her shudder. Although she despised him, the likeness between them wasn't far off. After all, they both abused children.

"No, I couldn't imagine they would," she said. "I know I wouldn't. If I were them I would be relieved that I was gone. I have offered them nothing but grief."

She didn't like admitting the truth. It was unnatural. She ran stiff fingers through her wet hair. A handful fell out and entangled her fingers.

She stared at it for a moment, unsure of what she held. Her concern made her repeat the process and another cluster came out. Panic consumed her and she began to pull clumps of hair out.

"You can stop," Sariel said. "There is hardly anything left."

She paused in her frenzy and felt that only a few random patches of hair remained. She tugged on another clump.

"What is this?" she said and held up the hair.

"I told you that you were dying and that your body would transform."

She stood there, wordless, the hair falling from her fingers.

"We don't have time to waste," he said. "The last we saw of your interaction with Wilson was when you told him that you were going to come and see Beau."

12

A FRESH START

The past.

The alarm next to Cailean's bed jarred her awake. She fumbled for the off button, sat up, rubbed her eyes, and stretched. A long yawn accompanied a moan that opened her mouth fully and she pushed the blankets off of her legs and stood.

Last night after she hung up the phone with Wilson, she realized she had been in service of her resentment all of these years. She had allowed it to take control over her and alter her behavior for reasons she could not understand. It had a firm hold over her and it had had it for so long that she couldn't remember being without it. The idea of wanting to rid herself of it worried her because whenever she challenged it in the past she would lose several days to binge drinking and, more recently, even attempt suicide.

But none of those things mattered anymore. Wilson had been right; this was about Beau and it always should have been. It was a brand new day and she was going to take a stand against it—even if it killed her.

Out of the bedroom and down the stairs she went with a purpose. She ignored the voice that told her not to do what she was about to do, that she was making a mistake. But that was like her worry of leaving her dysfunction behind and it no longer mattered. She made up her mind and there was no going back.

Ten minutes later she poured the last beer into the sink and watched it drain away. A belief that she could actually defeat the bad behavior by sheer will filled her with a newfound strength that brightened her path and emboldened her resolve. The drinking would stop and she knew the first and most difficult step in casting the addiction to the side would be to remain sober and deal with her emotions, no matter how difficult, with a clear mind.

"I'll starve you to death," she said. "Give you nothing to feed off of."

The habit of speaking aloud had progressively increased as her addiction deepened. She would speak to it often as if it were there, standing in front of her. For the longest time she believed it had made things easier for her because it readily turned the blame for her inadequacies towards everyone else. And she felt she owed it because of that.

"I want you away from me," she had said last night before she went to bed. "This time I mean it. I've given enough to you and now it is time I do for me."

Her declaration didn't come without a substantial price. The demon inside had awoken her frequently throughout the night and had demanded satisfaction. It was unrelenting and it tried to use her fatigue as a weapon. And there were many times she wanted to give in to its persistent demands so she could get some rest. But with great resolve and determination she rolled over, pulled the blanket over her head, and resisted it.

"You can do this," she said, and left the kitchen. She walked into the bathroom with her overnight victory fresh on her mind. Armed with some much-needed confidence, she readied herself to see Beau. She chose her favorite pair of blue jeans and a knit turtleneck sweater. When she neatened her clothing and checked herself in the mirror, she sighed at what she saw. The overnight battle had left its mark. Bags that hung beneath her eyes required multiple layers of foundation to cover.

"The first night," she said into the mirror and smiled. Her teeth had yellowed and the lines on her face had deepened tremendously over the past few years. These were details she either missed or chose to ignore; she couldn't remember and identified the realization as a distraction she could do without.

She exited the bathroom, walked to the closet, and put on her coat. A wool cap with a pompom would serve her well against the bitter cold outside, and she grabbed her car keys.

Although her nerves brought some doubt to the surface, her focus remained on Beau and her need to change. This had to be done and she would stay the course no matter how difficult it proved to be.

Cailean stuffed her trembling hands into her coat pockets and tried to convince herself that the shiver was just a reaction to the bitter cold. But the knot in her stomach told her otherwise.

The cold air burned her lungs and forced her to take short breaths. Patches of ice on the walkway required her to carefully navigate her way towards the front door. As she drew closer to the house, the odd feeling of being back home gave her pause. After all, this was where she had tried to ignore whatever was wrong with her and to live a normal life. Getting married and starting a family seemed the best way to insert a sense of regularity into her life. But she couldn't control forever what she had managed to momentarily suppress. It nagged her constantly and often showed itself through bouts of extreme aggression, days of profound sadness, and a constant lack of energy.

"Beer and wine," she said and continued on with a slow approach. "That's what kept it quiet."

How about a drink then?

"No."

Are you sure?

"Go away."

One wouldn't hurt. It might even relax you some.

"I said to leave me alone, I need to do this."

You're going to regret this decision.

She hadn't been to the house since Wilson told her to leave and she'd had no intentions of ever returning again. And yet here she was, standing at the front door with a welcome mat beneath her feet.

She felt anything but welcome.

To defy the voice that begged to reason with her, she knocked on the door.

What have you done?

An overwhelming desire to run filled her completely. She didn't want to be in that awkward moment of silence that assuredly would imbed itself between her and Wilson when he answered the door. It would transpire the instant he realized that she showed up against his wishes. The disappointment on his face would be easy to see and it would dig up harbored feelings she would rather remain undisturbed.

But before she could organize a plan, the door swung open and Wilson looked at her.

"Hello, Wilson," she said, and offered a gentle smile.

His confusion distorted his face and drained the color from it. He looked over his shoulder and then back at her. "What are you doing here?" he said, and stepped out of the house and pulled the door closed.

"I've come to see Beau."

He folded his arms across his chest. Dressed in a t-shirt, sweatpants, and socks, he was exposed to the bitter chill.

"I told you not to come here," he said. "I don't want you seeing him."

"But I need to see him," she said.

"He is really upset with you. You should go."

"I know he's upset with me and I don't blame him. I've been something far worse than horrible to him and I don't know if I even deserve another chance, but I have to try. I didn't drink last night to prove to you that I can do this."

"You didn't drink for one night and this proves you can change?"

"You don't know what obstacles I had to overcome. It's a start, and to me that is worth something."

"It is, Cailean, but you need to be sober for a few months or maybe a year. An alcoholic doesn't get better in one night. This will be a lifelong struggle for you."

"I know it will. It already has been. But I didn't come here for this. I know what I'm up against and I'm prepared to go all the way with it. The reason I came today is to see Beau."

"And I told you on the phone last night that I didn't think that was a good idea. I told you not to come."

"You were willing to let me see him yesterday, but now that I am here you think you're going to turn me away? What was it you said about not letting anything stop you? You said something about a waterfall and all of the snow in the world. Does that sound familiar to you? That is how I am today, right now, and you're an obstacle I plan on getting around."

He shivered and rubbed his arms. "That wasn't a talk to try and pump you up and get you over here. I meant it when I told you I didn't want you to come."

"I have every right to be in that house. I only left because of Beau. I knew he deserved better and now I am ready to give him that."

"You're delusional. If you don't leave I will call the police and have them remove you."

"Go right ahead, let your son see you do that to his mother, to the person he's been waiting to see for so long. I'll be sure to tell him that you're trying to keep us apart."

Wilson's expression contorted into complete disgust. "You're dirty, you know that? You've been gone all this time and I see nothing has changed with you."

"I disagree," she said. "I am here. I made myself a promise that I was going to see him today, and that is the first promise I've kept in a long time. I wasn't going to allow alcohol to get in the way of that anymore so I dumped it all down the drain. Now if I have to step past you to get to see him, I will. You couldn't fathom how hard I had to fight to gather the nerve to come here and do this sober. Especially knowing I was going to be in your crosshairs the moment you opened that door. Whether you agree or not, it doesn't matter to me. I want you to say what you have to say and then step aside so I can see Beau. I've been through a lot to get here and I'm not going to leave without seeing him."

Wilson raised his chin to her. "When was the last time you looked at yourself in the mirror?" He stared and raised a brow. "Christ, Cailean, you look like you've aged ten years since I last saw you."

She looked away. She knew she should have spent more time readying herself. Maybe that would have hampered his ability to criticize.

"Do you want to scare your son looking like that?"

"No," she said. "I just want to see him so I can remember the reason why I need to clean up and stay that way."

"I'll send you photos of him. Place them all around your house and use them as motivation to get healthy."

"Dad?" they heard from the other side of the door.

Wilson stiffened. "Damn it, Cailean, this is what I was trying to avoid. I want you to keep quiet," he said and pushed the door open enough to fit his head inside the house. "Yes, Beau, is everything OK, buddy?"

"Why are you standing outside?"

Wilson laughed. "I'm just having a talk with someone. I'll be inside in a minute."

"Is that Mom? Is she out there with you?"

"Why don't you watch some television or something? I'll be inside in a moment, OK?"

"I want to see her."

"Please, Beau, do as I ask and go inside and watch some television."

"I've been waiting to see her. Can she come in?"

Wilson sighed, hung his head, and then looked back through the door at Beau. "OK, Beau, yes, your mother is here."

"Tell her to come inside, Dad. It's cold outside. C'mon. Please?"

Wilson looked over his shoulder and gave her that look, the one that showed his displeasure. He pushed the door open and Cailean and Beau locked eyes.

"Mom!" he shouted and smiled.

She stood perfectly still and her eyes filled with tears. There he was, looking back at her with tangible pleasure. He didn't give her an accusing gaze or an awkward look like she had expected. All she saw was pure satisfaction and she didn't know what to do with it.

"Mom," Beau said and pushed the joystick forward on his power wheelchair. He stopped at the threshold of the doorway and opened his arms. "I can't believe you are here!"

She stepped forward and embraced her son. Squeezing him tight, she planted a kiss on his soft cheek. "I am so sorry for everything I've done to you and your father."

"It's OK, Mom. I'm just glad you're here."

Cailean looked up at Wilson, who was fighting away tears she knew were from the threat of her being there, cracking the wall of protection he'd built around himself and Beau.

She pulled away from Beau and looked at him with clear, wide eyes. "You've gotten so big. And look at you driving around in that fancy thing."

"I like it a lot," he said, backed up, and spun the chair in a tight circle. "Dad said you guys got it for me to make it easier to get around. Thank you, Mommy, I love it."

She looked at Wilson and the humiliation reddened her face more than the cold. She didn't help him with Beau and hadn't since the accident. And yet he gave her credit for things she didn't deserve in an attempt to preserve her relationship with her son when all she ever did was lie and manipulate to get her next buzz.

"I needed to stop by and tell you that I love you and that I'm going to do better from now on," she said. "You're growing up so fast and I realize that I don't want to miss that. Not for another moment."

"You sound like you're getting ready to leave already. Are you?" He sat erect and he reached for her. "You can't go, not yet!"

"I need to, honey. But I will come back real soon, OK?"

"No, it's not OK. You don't need to leave! You just got here. Tell her, Dad." Beau took hold of her hand and squeezed tight. His grip was strong and desperate and he stared at his father.

Cailean squatted down in front of him, kissed his hand, and looked into his eyes. "I will come back, Beau. From now on I'm going to keep my promises to you."

"No," he said, and looked at his mother. "You are here now and I want you to stay." He looked at his father. "Dad, tell her she can stay for a while longer!"

"No, Beau, your mother is right," Wilson said. "She needs to get better first. But as long as she tries and continues to improve, she can come back as much as she wants."

"No!" Beau shouted. "I want her to stay, and if she can't stay, I want to go with her."

Wilson stepped forward and reached to break Beau's hold on Cailean. "You know that's not going to happen. You need to let her go."

"No, Dad, I never ask for anything. All I want to do is spend some time with her. If you don't let me, I'll never talk to you again."

Cailean looked at Wilson. He stared at Beau, visibly shocked at his son's outburst. She looked at Beau and he glared back at his father, unblinking.

"Can you give us a few minutes alone, Beau? I need to talk to your mother in private."

"Please, Dad," he said and let his mother's hand go. Tears fell from his reddening eyes. "Don't do this. This is all I ever wanted, and I've wanted it for a really long time."

"Just a moment, OK, Beau? She's not going to leave without us talking to you first, I promise. I just want to talk to her about adult things."

Beau backed out of the hallway and the quiet hum of his motorized wheelchair faded away.

Wilson leaned against the wall, closed his eyes, and drew a deep breath. He exhaled slowly. "You see what your coming here has done, right? You're going to disappoint him again because there is no way I'm letting him go anywhere with you."

"I didn't ask him to go anywhere," she said. "I didn't say anything when you asked me not to. I'm trying to be good in this, Wilson. This is his idea because it is what he wants to do. And do I need to remind you that you're the one who told me that this—" she swirled her hand in the air, "—isn't about you or me. This is about him. And if he wants to come by my house for the day, then he should be allowed to come. Who knows, if you don't let him, he might hate you as much as he hates me. At least you will finally know how that feels. So I'm going to tell him if he wants to come over that I'm OK with it, but that it is up to you."

"If your apartment is as small as you've said it is, then you couldn't possibly accommodate his wheelchair. Besides, you don't have any of the necessary equipment to properly care for him."

"Like what?"

"Ramps to get him in and out of the house."

"I don't need ramps. I can carry him in." She thought for a moment. "I'll take his regular wheelchair. I'm sure you still have it as a backup, don't you?"

Wilson nodded.

"That will work fine and it will be easy enough for me to transport it," she said.

Wilson looked at his feet and rocked on his heels. He rubbed the graying stubble on his chin. "My God," he said and laughed nervously. "I can't believe I'm actually considering this. I want this so badly for the both of you, but I'm not happy I've been put into this position."

"Stop being so dramatic, Wilson. Everything is going to be fine. Besides, it will be nice to show him where I live and to have some one-on-one time with him. If you want, I'll only have him over for a few hours and then I'll bring him back."

He nodded and closed his eyes. "Fine." He looked at her and everything about his expression was serious. "I just hope this decision doesn't come back to haunt me."

"It won't." She smiled big. "And if it makes you feel any better, you can call him every half hour or fifteen minutes to check in on him, I don't mind."

"All right. I want you to call me as soon as you get him to your house. I want to know that you've arrived safely."

"Fine. Just remember that the roads are far from perfect and it will take me a bit longer than usual to get home."

"And you need to make sure you put him on the toilet every fifteen minutes to a half hour. He has this thing about going in his diapers. It's a lot of work, but it is helping with his confidence."

"Every half hour? I've got it covered, no problem."

"I don't know if you remember, but taking care of him is hard work. This isn't going to be a picnic for you."

"I'm not scared," she said.

He studied her face. "If at any time you've had enough, you call me and I will come and get him."

"Thank you, but everything is going to be fine."

13

RESPONSIBILTY AND THE MASK

Present day.

"I am almost certain I am the reason Beau was in that wheelchair," Cailean said. "When we looked at each other I could feel my guilt and shame trying to surface. But something within held the emotions back and reminded me that they weren't useful and that I shouldn't show weakness."

"What do you think would happen if you ignored that thing inside?"

"Bad things," she said. "Very bad things."

"It has made you dependent upon it and you aren't strong enough to escape its hold."

"I know now that those thoughts and feelings come from the same thing that feeds me lies and allows me to borrow excuses in exchange for my constant misery. To think that I resisted it overnight only to discover I brought it back home to them again."

Her eyes glowed with disgust and she sat in the chair.

"I am wicked on the inside and it repulses me," she said. "Although I didn't see blame in Beau's eyes, I can't stop thinking it was there, hiding behind his desperate smile. Because, like my shame, for him, the memory of what I did to him will always remain."

"You have been looking for something within that boy that just doesn't exist," Sariel said.

"Because I can't see it doesn't mean it is not there."

"Beau never blamed you for anything."

"He should have if what I'm feeling is true."

"All he has ever wanted was to feel loved by his mother."

She raised her brow and tried to recall a memory where she showed him love. The memory wasn't there.

"Why else do you think he would cling to you so desperately?" Sariel said.

She touched her own numb hand in remembrance of his firm grasp. "I don't know," she said.

"It's because he wanted you to love him more than anything else, that's why. I heard him praying, wishing with all of his heart for you to come back to him. He didn't ask to walk again or ask to bring you and Wilson back together. All he wanted was your approval of him, for what he was. You couldn't give him that because the hate you've carried around with you for so long has soured your soul and stifled your compassion. You stink—even to me."

Cailean lifted her chin to the comforting touch of newly falling flurries. The space outside her mind seemed quiet and peaceful and she wished she could escape the chaos within to embrace the serenity for only a moment.

"I love that boy," she said, and that was the truth. "I don't know why I'm incapable of showing him that or why I'm such a monster."

"You have always reveled in your guilt and shame. And you have done so since you were a child. It has allowed you to be angry and it has provided you with the perfect excuse for your bad behavior. You are tainted—a virus, like Wilson figured you to be."

Cailean sneered at the dark, beating pulse all around her that suddenly turned ugly. "It's not like I'm proud of the things I've seen today. What I was has cost me a great deal, too!"

"What has it cost you that you didn't willingly pay?"

"I despise you for what you are doing to me," she said.

She remembered Sariel's white glassy eyes that looked like emotionless marbles. She wondered: What did they know of her pain? Her grief was personal and unique.

"And what about the cost everyone around you had to pay?" he said. "What of them?"

The snowfall intensified and simultaneously her irritation turned into indignation. She pounded her chest with her fist. "You don't think I can feel that there is an emptiness inside of me? It is a dark and lonely path I travel and I don't believe there is a light bright enough to illuminate it!"

"Even the darkest, most desolate of places can be lit. Even if only for a moment."

"Why do you torment me with riddles?" She fought to get her heavy, wet shirt off. She stood in her bra. "Go ahead, look inside! Pull me apart and tell me my pain isn't genuine."

She snarled like an animal making a final stand against her carnivorous hunter. But the stillness that followed stayed until she calmed. She put her shirt back on and felt silly about her outburst. Reminded of a child throwing a tantrum, she walked the perimeter of light. "Don't you understand that what you're doing to me is provoking?"

"Your inner turmoil is ripe and volatile, Cailean. I cannot deny that is what is responsible for attracting me to you."

Her face distorted at the mention of it.

"Inner pain that is so intense and screams out for help with such desperation is hard to ignore," he said. "Out of all the people in need, yours is the one that has been the loudest and has yelled the longest."

The idea of him following her around the circle of light the same way he had before disturbed her.

"How long have you been watching me?" she said.

"Do you remember the vision of lilies?"

The memory was there, but unfinished. She believed she knew the ending, but she wanted to know for sure. After attempting to move back into it without Sariel having to trigger it, she soon gave up her search.

"Yes, I remember," she said. "But not enough of it."

Sariel laughed. "Well then, perhaps you need something to stimulate your recollection? Very well . . ."

A second black box slid into the light and came to rest at her feet.

"Take this box to the table, place it next to the first one, and open it. Inside, you will find out what you really are like deep down inside. Because what is inside there is the moment that defined you, captured by me for you to see. I've held onto it all this time for this very moment."

She chuckled in doubt and lifted the box without hesitation. It was heavy and she struggled to place it on the table. Ends of an elaborate black silk bow were easy to see. She gave them a gentle tug that unraveled the knot elegantly. The black wrapping required a detailed examination to locate the seam, and when she found it she peeled it away and a plain brown box was all that remained.

Apprehensive, but unable to resist the need to open it, she drew a deep breath and grasped the lid with stiff fingers. Lifting it, her eyes widened but her expression sullied. The light above her head, as power-ful and as bright as it was, didn't illuminate the contents of the box. The pitch-black held within the square matched what was beyond her circle of light perfectly.

Submerging her hand into the uninviting maw, the sting of its touch mimicked that which Sariel's stroke had left on her chin. Refusing to give into the desire to pull away, she discovered something big and heavy lying flat on the bottom. She took hold of it and strained her muscles as she withdrew it.

She stared at it for a moment and tried to figure out what she held.

"Turn it over and look at it," Sariel said.

She rotated it and jerked in surprise. A forceful shriek erupted from her opened mouth and she tossed the heavy thing to the floor. It was some type of mold of Mr. Hagen's face, the man that had tracked her down in the lily garden and grabbed her by the ankles. The porcelain cast split in half. The crack went around the left side of the mouth, across the bridge of the nose, and through the right eye.

"It is his death mask," Sariel said.

"Why would you mold his face and show it to me?"

"So you could see what he looked like in his final moments."

"Damn him," she said in a blind rage and picked up the smaller half of the mask, lifted it over her head and slammed it on the tabletop. It shattered and blended perfectly into the snowy floor.

"Yes," Sariel said. "Damn him."

14

A WHITE LIE

The past.

Mr. Hagen pulled Cailean out of the thicket by her ankles.

"No!" she screamed. "Get your hands off of me!" She kicked and clawed at the dirt.

"Stand up on yer own two feet!" he said.

He picked her up and set her down.

"Look at what you've done to my lilies!"

She stared into his wide eyes, filled with rage. The overpowering stench of body odor filled her nostrils and she turned away.

"Look at me when I'm talking to you!"

She took a small step back, but the thicket blocked her way.

"I want you to look at what you've done," he said.

She looked down the path she'd been running and almost every single one of the four-foot flowers leaned over, their stems split. The disappointment that she didn't get them all made her frown.

"Why would you cut down my lilies?" he said.

"I didn't do that," she said. "I don't know how that happened."

"Is that so?"

He watched her closely.

He took out a cigar and lit it. Three quick puffs and he bent at the waist and looked into her eyes. "Then what was it you were doing when I shouted your name?"

"I wasn't doing nothing! I didn't even hear you call my name like you say you did."

"Then why did you try and hide after I shouted out to you?"

"I wasn't hiding. I was playing and I fell."

"You were playing?"

She nodded.

"I don't like what I see in your eyes," he said. "Something ain't right with you."

She shrugged.

"Your dress is covered in dirt. Your mother is going to tan your hide for ruining your Sunday's best."

She inspected her clothes and saw the stains. "I have to get home and clean up."

She motioned to step past him, but he blocked her way.

"I don't want you going anywhere just yet."

He knelt and looked around the undergrowth he had pulled her from. She could see him crane his neck from side to side.

He stood and held up two sickles for her to see. "Then what were you using these for?"

She shrugged again. "I wasn't using them because I ain't never seen those before."

"You sure are trouble, child. If I were to show these to your father do you think he'd recognize those as belonging to him?"

"I don't know, it's like I said, I've never seen them before."

"That's your story and you're going to stay with it?"

"It's the truth," she said and stepped on a bug that dared cross her path. "Besides, how should I know what kinda tools he's got? I'm not allowed in the toolshed and he made me promise I wouldn't go in there."

"Is that so?"

She smiled.

"What causes you to behave the way you do, Cailean?"

"I didn't do nothing wrong," she said.

With a look of discontent and a shake of his head, he said, "I'll never get the truth from you. Where are your parents right now?"

She hesitated. "They went to the store and they won't be home for at least another hour."

"I think you're lying because that is all you seem to do. Now tell me, are they home right now?"

"No! Go ahead and look if you don't believe me," she said. She waved her hand in the air and tried to disperse the cigar smoke.

He rubbed his chin and puffed on his cigar. "I don't know why they insist on leaving you home alone when you do nothing but cause trouble. This is the second time this week you've destroyed things of mine and now you're going to have to answer for it."

She glared at him. "I already told you I didn't do nothing to your stuff!"

"Go on," he said and stepped aside. "Get outta here. You're destroying my livelihood and I won't stand for it anymore. I'll be over your house around suppertime to speak to your parents. That should give you plenty of time to come up with an excuse. You better make it a good one."

She hesitantly stepped around him and watched him out of the corner of her eye.

"I know everyone is struggling, but there's got to be repercussions for your bad behavior or you'll grow up to be a no good bum."

"That'll still be better than what you do," she said and continued to watch him. When she created enough distance, she ran as fast as she could through the field of lilies and around the side of his house, across the street, and into her house.

"Mom!" The tears came quick and her mind worked fast.

Her mother met her a few feet into the doorway. Cailean was in full hysterics, crying so hard she could barely breathe.

"Cailean, honey, what is it?"

She tried to speak but the words were indecipherable.

"I need you to calm down, honey," her mother said. She rubbed her back and hugged her. She brought her daughter into the kitchen and looked over her daughter's filthy hands, stained dress, and muddy shoes.

"Were you up in the tree again? Did you fall and hurt yourself?"

"No," she said and shook her head, her hair whipping from side to side.

"Tell me what happened. Please, baby, you're scaring Momma."

"Cailean?" her father said. He appeared by the back door and the bright day's sun cast him in shadow. "You need to answer your mother and tell her what's going on."

She calmed herself as she watched her father move into the house. He was a big man and was very quiet. He worked hard all day long and she hardly ever saw him. Providing for the family was what he always did.

Sweat soaked his shirt and he wore his field hat with a bandana pinned to the back to protect his neck from the hot day's sun. He removed his hat and watched her carefully. Concern covered his tanned face.

"What happened, darling?"

He had been working in his own lily fields, tending to the harvest he readied to pot so he could sell. He reeked, too, but his smell didn't bother her.

"I did something terrible today, Daddy," she said. "I went across the street to Mr. Hagen's. I went to see his lilies."

"Aww, dammit, Cailean." He slapped his hat against his thigh. "You went back over there after what happened with him the other day? Why would you go and do such a thing? Do you know what trouble this can cause us?"

"Shh, let her speak," her mother said.

"Daddy is right. I shouldn't have gone over there," she said, and the tears continued to flow, breaking down her composure. "I just wanted to compare his against ours to see how much we might get against his stock."

"No, honey, you let the buyers decide that," he said.

"I know how important it is that we sell our stock this year . . . that our farm depends on it. But all I was doing was looking, I swear."

"So why are you covered in dirt?"

She cried hard. Her face was as red as an apple and she wiped her tears with her dirty, trembling hands.

"Please, Daddy, don't be mad at me." Smudges of dirt hid her freckles.

"Why would I be mad at you?"

"Because I went over there when I knew I shouldn't. And . . . I don't want to say it because I'm afraid of what might happen."

"Why would you be afraid? Did he threaten you or something?"

Cailean stopped her tears and looked at him in the eyes. Devoid of emotion, she said, "No, he did something much worse than that to me."

"Worse?" He dropped to a knee and took his daughter's small hand into his calloused grasp. "What do you mean, 'worse'?"

"He forced me to my knees and unzipped his pants."

"He did what?"

"Oh my God!" her mother said and she started a frantic search for the phone.

"I don't want to hear any more," he said, and stood. His movement was robotic and his demeanor changed to make room for the obvious, unspeakable rage that filled him.

"He told me he could make your life hell because of what I did, and he said if I didn't do as he said he'd say I damaged his crops. I ran away as fast as I could."

Blank faced and clearly detached from the moment, Cailean's father exited the kitchen.

"Hank?" her mother said. "Don't do anything stupid. Let me call the police and let's let them handle it."

He apparently didn't acknowledge his wife's words. Inside the hallway closet he removed a shotgun and exited the house.

"Mom?" Cailean said, and she thought she might have gone too far. She ran to her mother's side. "Daddy, please don't go over there!"

"Hank!"

As he walked across the street, Cailean saw him check to see if the gun was loaded. When he arrived at Mr. Hagen's front door, he knocked hard, took a step back, and aimed his weapon.

When Mr. Hagen opened the door, Cailean could see the flash from the muzzle and simultaneously, see the old man get blown back inside his house. The piercing sound of the gun blast quickly followed and she watched her mother run out of the house and across the street. Grounded by her lie and what it caused, she began to cry.

"Hank, what have you done?" her mother screamed.

15

KEEPING SECRETS, NO MATTER WHAT

Present day.

"Your father spent the rest of his life in prison, believing with all of his heart and soul that he was being punished unjustly. You put him there because you were a coward," Sariel said.

"But I was only a child."

"He thought the man he killed was a terrible person that had committed an unspeakable act against his child. In that moment he went to get his gun, something inside his mind snapped and there was no going back. He didn't plan his malice like you did."

"I can't be held responsible for that. I was scared and didn't know what to do."

"You weren't scared. You were . . . emerging."

The insinuation inflamed her ire and she pushed her fingers into her ears to try and elude it.

"Stop telling me these things. What's done is done and I cannot change it," she said.

"Cold and calculating, that's what you are. I often wondered how he would have felt if he knew the truth."

His gruff voice penetrated her barricade, and to her dismay, she heard every word.

"Do you remember the first time you saw your father through the glass inside the prison?"

"Yes," she said and the memory came as he spoke it. The concrete and steel and the loud bangs and tight handcuffs seemed so inhumane. He appeared tired and weak and she couldn't stand to see it. Apprehension, regret, denial, and guilt were in a tug-of-war with her emotions.

"What was he doing?"

She lowered her hands away from her ears.

"He was holding the phone, waiting for me to take it from my mother so he could talk to me."

"What were you feeling?"

"I was frightened. I didn't want to talk to him, but I knew I must or he'd somehow know about my deception."

"He was locked in a cage for the rest of his life and armed guards surrounded him constantly. What were you frightened of?"

"Anyone finding out the truth—especially him. I wanted to tell him and almost did, but I couldn't."

"Why?"

"Because then everyone would know it was my fault."

"During the trial they said he had gone on a rampage; that he had snapped over Mr. Hagen's success and his own failures. They charged him with premeditated murder and your father pleaded guilty to those charges."

"I know he did."

"Why do you think he did that?"

"To try and protect me," she said. "He didn't want them knowing I went over there."

"When you took the phone from your mother at the prison, what happened?"

"She encouraged me to talk to him because she knew I was afraid."

"What did she say?"

"I remember it like it happened yesterday. She got down on her knees, hugged me, and whispered gently that my father loved me and that he needed to hear my voice."

"And?"

"My father told me that I didn't have to worry about anyone hurting me ever again and that he loved me more than anything in the whole world."

"And what did you say back to him?"

"Nothing. I couldn't speak."

"Because you didn't feel love back, did you?"

"I was inside of a prison!"

"Yes, and he was kept in a room no bigger than the area of light you occupy now. He did that for you. He sacrificed the rest of his life and you didn't say anything back to him?"

"No, I didn't." She swallowed hard. "I just couldn't. It kills me inside to have to live with that, but what was I going to say to him?"

"What do you think you should have said?"

Perspective pushed her apprehension, regret, and denial aside.

"I'm sorry," she whispered. "That's what I should have told him."

"But you didn't because you weren't sorry either. And you're still not," he said. "You can't fool me."

The burden of knowing the truth she faced was absolute hell, and as Sariel had said when she first arrived, she was going to have come face to face with who she was. She couldn't help but think: What purpose did her life serve?

"You're emotionless and heartless," he said.

"I know I am," she said.

"By the age of fifteen you had recited your tale of the events from that day so many times that you began to believe it was actually true. Your ability to manipulate people became your first and strongest addiction. You eventually convinced your mother that you were frightened of your father and that you had suffered nightmares about his evil ever since the day of the shooting. But that wasn't true, was it?"

"No, it wasn't."

"Then why?"

"Because every time I saw him it reminded me of what I had done and I wanted to put that behind me."

"So you left him to rot so you could ease your guilty conscience?"

"I had to or it would have driven me crazy."

"And you think the decisions you made were from a sound mind?"

She didn't want to answer that question.

"You should have been locked up in an institution. Instead, you dared to start a family."

"I wanted so badly to be normal."

"And no matter how hard you tried, you couldn't be," he said.

"Did you see my father after he died?"

"He was so lost and confused in his death state," he said. "I remember him asking me over and over again why his wife and child left him to wither away after he sacrificed so much for them."

Although she knew it wouldn't do any good, she turned away. She tried to fight the image of her father on his knees, still begging to understand. But no matter where she turned, Sariel's voice came as if he was standing in front of her, forcing her to hear what he had to say.

"And your mother turned to alcohol to try and drown her sorrows," he said. "That is where you got the idea. The hole that day had left in her soul could never be repaired and you knew it. She became a nuisance to you and the moment you could get away from her, you did."

"She was always depressed and sulking in her loss of my father," Cailean said. "I couldn't take it anymore."

"You left her alone, knowing her final act was inevitable."

"Yes I knew, and I didn't want to be around to see it."

"Her death was planned and it was as a direct result of your actions. She did it to escape you and to be with your father. She suspected there was something wrong with you and feared what you had become."

"That's just not true."

"Yes, it is the truth. When I took her to the judgment door, I could see how your deceit had taken all of her will and pulverized it. She had become a shadow of her former self."

The remaining half of the death mask stole Cailean's attention and she couldn't help but notice how the eye had been clamped shut and the mouth was pulled back in an image of intense pain. It had become apparent that the mask had been cast only moments after Mr. Hagen had taken the shotgun blast to the abdomen.

"You would not be here if you would have acknowledged the voice of reason that begged for your attention instead of ignoring it."

"Stop it!" She slammed her fist on the tabletop, his words a welcomed distraction.

"Why? Because you realize you chose to embrace your ugly side and it doesn't like to be known?"

She didn't like what he said and kicked snow at the darkness. "Shut up!"

"Or what?"

Frantic, Cailean searched for something and settled her attention on the other chair that had been left undisturbed since she arrived. She took hold of it and lifted it onto the tabletop. Centering it, she swiftly jumped onto the table.

"I don't need to listen to this!" she said.

"But the thing that was the ugliest is what made you the most comfortable, isn't it? No matter how much you despised it, it was still better than having to face the truth."

Climbing on the chair, she reached her hand up and stood on her tiptoes. Stretching higher and groaning with the strain, she tried to grab the light.

"I want this damn thing turned off," she said.

"It's not you who wants the light off," Sariel said.

"I won't allow you to keep me confined to this space so you can continue to dissect me."

"All of that effort to conceal such a thing must be so tiresome."

"I won't!"

She jumped up and grabbed for the light source. The chair slid out from underneath her feet and she crashed down on the table and fell to the floor. Pain free but dazed, she looked up at the light, panting, the rage inside her deep. Lying on her back and watching the wind tossing the snow around, she felt a sudden sense of peace within the pandemonium.

"You must desire a break from it," Sariel said. "Fret no longer, our time to confront what has been ailing you is drawing near."

16

IT ISN'T EASY

The past.

"I'm really happy Dad let me come to your house for part of the day," Beau said.

"I am, too. You did a great job convincing him," Cailean said with a mischievous smile.

"I meant what I said. I've missed you, Mom, and I want to see you more," he said with seriousness to his voice well beyond his years.

"Thank you, honey. I've missed you, too."

Beau had his face pressed against the chilled passenger side window and looked at the two-story apartment complex they approached. Snow-drifts were pushed against the walls and were as high as the ground floor windows. Long, sparkling icicles hung off of the eaves in a spectacular display of winter beauty.

"Is this where you live, Mom?" He tapped the window, pointing at the narrow development.

"It is," she said and laughed at his excitement. It was good to hear him acting like a kid. "This is where I live."

"It seems so far away from us."

"It's not that far. It has taken us a bit longer because of the weather."

"It is really nice though, Mom. It looks like it has an upstairs."

"You know, you're right, there is an upstairs."

"Oh," he said. "I wonder what it looks like up there."

"Well, maybe we can think of a way to get you up there. What do you think?"

"That sounds great!"

"Do you see that window up there?"

"That one?" he said, and tapped the glass again. A large window on the second floor protruded from the unit and appeared twice the size of an ordinary window.

"Yes, that's the one. That's in my bedroom. I'll bet you would be able to see the entire street the same way a bird does when they're flying around."

Beau's face brightened. "That would be so cool, Mom."

The car pulled into a short driveway and the ice popped and crunched underneath the wheels. Cailean watched as Beau craned his neck to see as much of the house and snow covered neighborhood as possible. She looked around, too; everything was white and glistening.

"So, what do you say?" Cailean said, and put the car in park. "Do you want to get inside and have a look around?"

"Yes!" He pumped his fist.

"All right, let's do this," she said and shut off the car. The bitter cold penetrated the interior instantly.

"Do you feel that already?" she said.

Beau nodded and gave pause to a swooping wind that shook the car. "Yeah, it is really cold out there."

"The cold is no match for us. I think I have a plan," she said. "I'm going to carry you inside and set you down on the couch. Then I'll run back out to the car and get your wheelchair and the bag your father packed before it can even touch us. What do you think?"

"I like it, Mom."

"Great," she said and opened the car door fully with a kick.

The intensity of the cold made her move fast. She hurried around the car, pulled open the passenger door and leaned into the vehicle.

"Put your arm around my neck and hold on tight."

He did as instructed and Cailean slid an arm underneath his legs and the other arm around his back. She lifted him out of the car and she hurried up the walkway.

"How are you doing?" she said.

He flexed his hands. "It's really cold out here. I can feel it on my face and hands."

"We'll be inside in a second."

She struggled to open the front door.

"Come on!" she said, and twisted the handle.

"But not my legs, Mom."

"What?" she said, and entered the house. She set him down on the couch.

"The cold. I couldn't feel it on my legs." He smiled.

"You're being silly," she said. "I want to get the rest of the stuff out of the car. I'll be back in a second."

"No, Mom, wait!"

She stopped. "What is it? Is everything OK?"

"I think you should take me to the bathroom first. I don't want to have an accident."

"I have to take you right this second? Can't it wait until after I get your chair and bag inside?"

He shook his head. "I don't think we should wait and I could already be done by the time you get back," he said. "Dad said to make sure I go every fifteen minutes to be on the safe side and I think we were in your car for way longer than that."

She sighed. "I wish you would have told me that when I went over the plan with you in the car. I probably would have elected to bring the wheelchair in first. That probably would have made more sense rather than my having to pick you up and carry you all around the house."

"I'm sorry, Mom."

"It's not a big deal," she said and messed his hair. "I'm just happy you're here."

She lifted him off of the couch and carried him towards the bathroom.

"So how would you and your father normally do this?"

"He would just put me down on the floor and I would do the rest myself."

She hesitated. "I don't want to leave you on the floor. That doesn't seem right."

Beau laughed. "It's OK, Mom. This is how we do it all the time."

"All right," she said and set him down on the bathmat in the center of the small bathroom. She straightened his legs. "Are you sure you don't need me to help you get onto the toilet?"

"Yes, I'm sure, Mom. I do this all the time and this is kind of private."

"If you need me I'll be right outside the door," she said.

"If you want to go and get the stuff out of the car, I'll be fine."

"No, I don't think I'm going to do that. I'll wait right here."

She stepped out of the bathroom and into the hallway. She closed the door halfway and leaned against the wall. The large mirror gave her the perfect vantage point to watch over him without his knowing.

Beau pulled his pants down and looked inside his diaper.

"Yes," he said and clapped his hands.

He army crawled across the floor and his limp legs dragged the bathmat along. Resting once he reached the base of the toilet, he placed one hand on the rim of the bowl and the other on the nearby bathtub. He lifted himself and swung his legs around the toilet and sat.

He rested his elbows on his knees and looked around the room. Moments later he looked between his legs.

"All right!" he said.

He planted a hand on the tub and sink and lifted himself off the bowl. As he lowered himself, his hand slipped off the tub and he fell to the floor with a heavy thump.

"Beau?" Cailean said, and threw the door open. She hurried to his side. "Oh my God, Beau, are you all right?"

He struggled to cover himself and tried to pull up his diaper.

"Mom, I'm not dressed!"

"It's OK, I'm not looking," she said and helped him cover up.

"My hand slipped."

She didn't want to say she saw the entire thing. "I knew this wasn't a good idea and I'm sorry I didn't listen to myself. I need you to be more careful!"

"I was being careful! The tub was wet and my hand slid off." He rubbed the back of his head. "Why didn't you dry it off if you knew I was coming over?"

"Did you hit your head?"

"It doesn't matter," he said, and turned away from her.

"You scared me half to death."

He scowled.

"Come on, sit up," she said and helped him do so.

She saw the filth from the floor on his hands and elbows and a wave of embarrassment swept over her. She had showered a few hours ago and that had made this accident her fault.

"Let me get your wheelchair out of the car and then I'll get you cleaned up."

He nodded his acceptance.

She exited the bathroom and paused when she got to the kitchen doorway. The cupboard that once held her booze beckoned her. It told her that if her frustration needed a reprieve it might have something that may have been overlooked.

"There's nothing in there. I made sure of it. This is a new day and a new start," she whispered and stepped into the kitchen. The urge to know if she might have missed something was strong.

"Mom, are you getting me my chair so I can get off this floor and get washed up?"

"Yes," she said, the distraction enough to squash her curiosity and force her out of the kitchen. "I'm going out now."

She went outside and barely noticed the cold. The idea that she almost gave in to the alcohol so soon left her frustrated.

"Stupid, stupid, stupid."

She balled her fist and pounded it into the palm of her hand.

"Why did you think you could beat it?"

She hated the fact that her addiction was more powerful than the care she had for her own son.

Opening the trunk, she grabbed the wheelchair and tried to pull it out, but it was stuck. Placing a foot on the bumper, she gave the chair a strong yank. It popped free and she stumbled backwards and fell into a snowdrift.

"Damn it!"

She jumped to her feet and brushed the snow off of her clothes, grabbed the frame of the chair, and dragged it up the walkway and into the house. She grappled with it and cursed herself for not paying better attention when Wilson showed her how to use it.

Once she figured it out, she rolled it down the hallway and found Beau waiting in the same spot she had left him.

"I'm sorry," she said. "I couldn't get it out of the trunk."

Beau laughed. "Your hair has snow in it."

She looked in the mirror and laughed at what she saw. A small pile of snow sat on top of her head. "I guess I lost my hat when I fell. Darn, I love those pompoms."

"You can go back outside and get it."

She shook her head. "I don't love them that much. It really is cold out there and I can barely feel my fingers."

Lifting him into the chair, Cailean positioned his feet on the footrests. "Are you comfortable?"

He nodded and she washed his hands and arms.

"I'm going to need you to remind me when I'm supposed to take you to the bathroom next."

"That's OK. I like to do it myself."

"No," she said and shook her head. "Absolutely not. I want to know when you're going. God forbid you fall again. You could be there for a long time before I even realized you were gone."

"I won't fall again."

"Please, Beau, just do as I ask."

He nodded.

"And I'm sorry about the mess in the house. I'm embarrassed you had to see it. I live alone and don't clean up behind myself as well as I should."

The doorbell rang.

"Would you like to watch some television so I can see who that is?"

"That's fine, Mom."

She backed the wheelchair out of the bathroom and the handrims scraped the walls. She groaned in displeasure and examined the deep lines that ripped through the paint.

"That's no big deal," she said and ignored her growing frustration. She moved Beau into the family room and slid the coffee table aside and centered the wheelchair to the television. The doorbell rang again and it was followed by a series of hard knocks.

"Hold on a second!" she shouted and turned on cartoons and purposely set the volume loud. The idea that Wilson might have followed her home to check on them didn't help with her changing mood. If he was outside that door she was going to give him a piece of her mind.

"I'll be back in a few minutes, sweetie. Do you need me to bring you anything when I return?"

"No, thank you, Mom."

She walked the hallway and seethed at the idea that Wilson gave her no trust whatsoever. She yanked the door open, and to her surprise,

Emerson stood there with his hands stuffed into his coat pockets and a ski cap pulled down tight around his big head.

"Emerson?" she said.

"It's really cold out here, Cailean." His breath stained the air and his bright red cheeks and nose confirmed his declaration.

"Yes, I know. My son is here and now is really not a good time for this." The cold penetrated her clothes and she pushed the door closed to a slit.

"You left the trunk of your car open and I closed it. You must have dropped this." He handed her the pompom hat.

"Thank you."

"If you allow me inside, what I have to say to you will only take a minute."

"What is it? What do you want?"

"Right now?" he stepped closer to the door. "I would like to warm up for a minute. I walked all the way here and now I have to turn around and walk all the way back."

"Why in the hell would you walk all the way here, in this?"

Emerson slapped his midsection. "Well, with some of the things you said, it really hit home. And honestly, it seemed like a good idea at the time."

She stepped aside and opened the door, offering him passage. "Just keep your voice down and make this quick."

"I will," he said and hurried into the house.

Cailean closed the door.

"And so much for you waiting to hear from me," she said.

He rubbed his hands together and blew into them. "I was worried about you and I didn't like the way things went between us. I wanted to come by and see how you were doing."

"I'm fine."

"Are you still mad?"

"I really haven't had much time to think about it. I've been busy trying to get myself right for Beau."

"That's great, it really is. I'm happy for you and support you one hundred percent." He smiled. "How did it go with Wilson?"

"Better than expected, I suppose. Beau's here with me, so that must tell you something."

Emerson unzipped his coat.

"What are you doing?" she said. "I already told you that you're not staying."

"I know that."

He reached inside his coat and withdrew a crumpled brown bag and held it out for her to take.

"Here, this is for you," he said.

"What is it?"

"A peace offering."

She wanted to turn away from him and tell him to get the hell out of her house, but she also wanted what was inside that bag.

"Now is not the best time for that," she said.

Her words were without conviction and she could hear it.

"No, I know it's not." He turned to the counter and placed the bag down. "But maybe later, after Beau goes, you might find it useful. I'm sure you threw everything you had away again and you'll be going crazy for some after he leaves for the night."

She wanted to tell him something to the contrary but didn't want him to take away what he had brought. She watched him walk to the door.

"If you would like some company, you could call me later on and I'll come over," he said.

She nodded. "Sure, OK."

Emerson zipped his coat, smiled at Cailean, and exited the house.

She looked at the bag and then looked down the hallway toward the family room. "Damn," she said and could envision Beau waiting for her. But he was quiet and really—what was one more minute?

Opening the bag, she removed two bottles of red wine and set them back down on the counter. She wanted a taste so badly she started to shake.

The phone rang next to her.

"Hello?"

"Cailean?" Wilson said, the anger in his tone palpable. "I thought you said you were going to give me a call when you got in?"

"I did . . . at least I intended to. The roads are really icy and it took me longer than I thought to get home. And it was a little more challenging getting Beau inside the house and settled."

"Did you take him to the bathroom yet?"

"Yes," she said.

"He didn't go in his pants, did he?"

"No, I don't think so."

"If he didn't say anything to you, then he didn't. That's good."

"Well I don't see what the big deal is anyway. He wears a diaper."

Wilson sighed. "We discussed this already. I told you it was going to be a lot of work and you said you were fine with it."

"I am fine with it. I was just saying."

"It's a phase he's in and it makes him happy. He's getting a little older now and is becoming more aware of what kids his age are supposed to do."

"I understand."

"Cailean, please don't make me regret this. I'm nervous about the whole thing to begin with and when you didn't call . . ."

"Everything is fine." The bottles of wine were a distraction and she turned her back to them. "And I know everything I have to do for him."

"Where is he now?"

She looked towards the hallway. "He's in his chair, warming up in front of the television." She felt a tap on her shoulder and turned, but no one was there. She glanced at the bottles. "I was getting ready to make him a cup of cocoa."

"Can I speak to him, please?"

She squeezed the phone and clenched her jaw. Stifling a need to protest his request with an unpleasant rebut, she tried to keep the frustration from her voice. "Sure, no problem."

He was babysitting her and impeding on her time with Beau. She walked down the hallway and felt the annoyance settle in her throat. It was a big lump that she tried to swallow.

"Your father would like to speak to you."

Beau's eyes lit up and he went to take the phone. Cailean moved it away and put her lips next to his ear. "Don't say anything about falling in the bathroom or the dirt. If you do, he won't let us hang out."

Beau nodded and she stood up and smiled. She placed the phone in his hand and went into the kitchen. Choosing a bottle of wine, she took it off the counter and took the corkscrew out of the drawer and opened the bottle.

There was no need for a glass. She put the bottle to her lips and drank until she was out of breath.

17

A BLACK BOX

Present day.

Cailean was dazed. Last she remembered she was on her back and looking up at the light after she fell from the table. The blizzard-like conditions had given her the peace she sought and now it was gone, replaced by a smothering silence. Somehow she had made it into the chair and sat comfortably with her elbows resting on the table. She craved the wine she drank before she was ripped back here to this brightly lit section of hell.

"Go on," Sariel said.

She flinched and held a hand over her racing heart.

"Open the box on the table," he said.

She searched the black but couldn't locate him. "Don't do that. Your voice is frightening and it goes right through me."

"The box," he said.

"What's in it?" she said.

"Ask me no other questions and just open it."

She hesitated. "The last time you made me do this I came out with a molded mask of the man my father killed. A mask you made after he died."

"Open the box."

Her hands pulled away the bow and she searched the paper for the seam. With haste, she pulled away the black wrapping and an identical brown box remained. Not wanting to give into her trepidation, she lifted the lid and tossed it aside. Reaching her hand into the abyss, she felt no effects of the darkness. It took her several moments to locate what lay inside at the very bottom.

When she withdrew her hand, she came out with a dirty, tattered stuffed animal that looked like a giraffe. She had no memory of it and was unable to understand why it made her hesitant. She felt uneasy while she stared at the threadbare cloth exterior.

"What is this?" she said and held it up for Sariel to see.

"Something more defining in your life than the event surrounding your mother, father, and Mr. Hagen."

"A stuffed animal was more defining than my father killing another man because of my lies? And my mother committing suicide because she feared what I was becoming?"

She laughed.

When she had withdrawn the death mask from the box its significance could be felt right away. But whatever secrets this mangy, fetid thing held, she no longer remembered or cared about it. She wondered if Sariel might have overestimated its significance.

"You may not know it, but I can see from here that you loathe it," he said.

"It's filthy," she said, and dropped it on the tabletop. "If I can't remember it, how important could it have been?"

She felt it was a waste of her time. Yet, without knowing why, she went back to it and ran her fingers over the stubby body and long thin legs.

"I am curious, though, why didn't I like it?" she said.

"Because it was loved and you always felt you were not," Sariel said.

"Are you telling me someone held affection for this mangy thing? How could someone love this, an inanimate stitched up sack of cotton . . . and I be jealous of it?"

Her doubt twisted her mouth.

"You admired your drink, didn't you?"

She pursed her lips and nodded. "I suppose."

"You despised what you couldn't understand."

"What does this stupid toy have to do with anything?"

"For the person that it belonged to? Everything!"

"Whose was it?"

"The answer is underneath your nose, contained within your repulsion. Search for it and you will find the answer you seek."

She picked it up and studied it closer. Hoping his words provided her with the proper clue, she brought the toy animal to her nose and sniffed. Pain filled her head and another memory came fast.

18

A DAY AT THE PARK

The past.

Cailean tugged on the bill of her pink Boston Red Sox baseball cap to help shield her eyes from the hot sun. Although she didn't care much for the sport, the embossed letter B was what had appealed to her. To her it meant *Bitch,* and that described her perfectly.

Her ponytail stuck out of the back of the hat and large sunglasses covered most of her face. She sat on a park bench that overlooked the large playground. Swings, slides, tunnels, ramps, and staircases split off in all directions. Woodchips covered the ground and a chain-link fence circumscribed the entire playground. The river ran parallel with the park and created the perfect backdrop. The waves that lapped the rocky shoreline produced a constant sloshing sound that she found comforting.

A gentle breeze lifted her hair and a father shadowing his young daughter kept her attention. The child ran around the massive structure and made the father appear clumsy and overly nervous with her every move. Cailean couldn't help but laugh at how winded and out of shape he was.

"Mom?"

Cailean ignored Beau.

"Mommy!"

"Don't raise your voice like that," she said and didn't offer him a look. "Go on and play. Go down the curly slide a few times with Rafi. I don't want to stay too long. I'm not feeling well."

She removed a water bottle from the inside pocket of her North Face jacket and twisted the cap off. Drinking two mouthfuls, she concentrated on the slow burn the vodka left behind as it descended her throat.

She had come to appreciate the feeling because no matter what war was being fought on the inside, the fiery sensation helped extinguish the disharmony for a short period of time.

"I said to go and play," she said.

"But I want you to come with me, Mommy," Beau said, and reached his hand out to her.

A certain level of satisfaction filled Cailean that she could disguise alcohol as water. It proved she was much smarter than everyone else around her.

"I just told you that I wasn't feeling well," she said and waved him away. "I've also told you that I don't want to stay too long and you're wasting time." She drained the rest of the vodka out of the bottle, stood, and stared at Beau. "Go now!" she said and pointed.

He ran away.

The nervous father walked by and flashed Cailean a cordial smile.

"Hello," he said.

Sweat glistened on his forehead and pockmarks rippled his cheeks. Although her eyes were hidden behind the tint of her glasses, she remained conscious enough not to give the direction of her stare away by the position of her head. Her eyes focused on the expensive watch strapped around his wrist. The Prada shoes, pants, and quilted down coat he wore screamed money.

"Hello to you," she said and understood that the Jaguar she parked next to when she arrived undoubtedly belonged to him. She tossed the empty bottle into the nearest trashcan.

"I'm Emerson," he said and held out his large hand for her to take.

"Cailean," she said and accepted his offering. She pumped his hand up and down and studied him. Without question she could move past the imperfections on his skin and all the extra weight he carried. For money she would do about anything.

The understanding that Wilson wouldn't be home for at least several more hours leapt into the forefront of her mind.

"It's very nice to meet you," he said.

She dismissed the irrational thought immediately. She wouldn't know what to do with Beau and didn't want to appear trashy. It wasn't every day that a seemingly rich man fell into her lap.

"Same here," she said and looked in the general area Beau might be in. She saw him standing in the center of the playground, sucking his thumb, and watching other children run around.

"It's perfect out here today, isn't it?"

"Yes, it is," she said and shoved her left hand into her jacket pocket. She thumbed her wedding ring and spun it on her finger.

"This is my daughter, Stacey," he said. "Stacey, say hello."

Stacey flashed Cailean a look of indignation, folded her arms across her chest, and then looked away.

"I'm sorry," he said. "She doesn't interact well with others."

"Don't worry about it. She's adorable," Cailean said, but really didn't think so. She looked like him—and for a girl, that wasn't a good thing.

She pointed at Beau. "And that handful over there is my son, Beau."

Emerson shielded his eyes from the sun. "Cute little guy." He looked at Cailean. "He looks a lot like you."

A smile parted her lips. "Thank you."

"Don't thank me for saying what is true," he said. "And the other one—I suppose he takes after his father?" Emerson said, smiling.

"Oh," Cailean laughed, "That grayish thing my son is carrying is Rafi, his stuffed giraffe. He used to be orange and white. Beau takes it everywhere with him."

"That's cute."

"It used to be. And you wouldn't be saying that if you got a whiff of it. Oh, and . . ." she patted the top of her head.

"Emerson felt the top of his head and found his sunglasses. "I've been looking all over the place for these. Don't mind me. I've been a little off today. It has been a stressful day."

"I'm sorry," she said, but really wasn't.

"Be careful, Stacey." He put the glasses on. "It is a beautiful day today. Please, allow me to take a picture of you and your son."

"No," Cailean said. "But thank you. I look a mess."

He took his cell phone out of his pocket and looked at her with doubt. "You're kidding me, right?"

She didn't want to seem pretentious and scare him off. "OK," she said. "Sure, why not? What could it hurt?"

She cupped her hands around her mouth. "Beau?"

He appeared from somewhere up high. His baseball cap was pulled low and made his ears stick out. Wedging his face between the bars, he looked down at his mother. "What?"

"Don't 'what' me. Come down here now!"

"But, Mom, I'm playing with Rafi."

"We're not leaving yet. I just need you to come here for a minute."

Beau hung his head as he walked the ramp and went down the stairs. He held Rafi by the neck and dragged him along. His long, skinny legs skipped down each step and bumped through the cypress mulch. The long body begged to be washed.

"Put Rafi down on the bench for a minute," Cailean said. "This nice man wants to take our picture."

He hugged Rafi and shook his head.

"Come on, Beau, just put him down. He'll be right there and you can get him the second we're done."

She took Rafi from him and set him down on the bench, wiped her hand on her pant leg, and squatted next to Beau. She removed her sunglasses and pulled him close. She pointed at Emerson and said, "Look right there and give me your best smile."

"That's great," Emerson said and took the picture. He studied the small screen on his phone. "It came out really nice."

"See, that wasn't so bad, was it?" she said to Beau.

"Not for me," he said, and ran to get Rafi. He walked to the playground stairs. "But it was very bad for Rafi. I don't like leaving him alone like that. He doesn't do that to me."

"He is really attached to that thing, huh?"Emerson said.

"Annoyingly so." She put on her sunglasses and removed a second bottle out from the inside jacket pocket. "And I'm surprised he put it down long enough for you to take a picture."

She took a drink.

"I think it's cute."

She didn't think so, but didn't want to say so again. She sat on the bench.

"Can I have your phone number?" he said.

"I'm sorry, what?"

Emerson held up his cell phone. "So I can send you your picture. What is your phone number?"

She gave him her number.

"Do you come here often?" she said.

"No," he said and looked at Stacey and saw that she was holding Beau's hand, leading him around. "Look at that."

"Now that's cute. Maybe they made friends today."

"I hope so," he said, and snapped another picture.

Cailean chuckled. "You look a little nervous with her."

"I am," he said, and seemed embarrassed by her saying so.

"I didn't mean anything by it. It's just the way you stay so close to her and you keep looking for her over your shoulder every second."

He smiled. "Yeah, I want to make sure she's doing OK."

"Now I think that's cute, too," she said.

"Yeah?" He smiled.

She nodded and drank some more. This guy was like putty in her hands already.

"This is the first time I've been able to take her out in a long time and I'm elated to see her having so much fun."

He looked at his watch.

"I only have a few minutes left with her before she has to leave," he said.

"I won't pry, I promise. And I won't keep you from your daughter," she said.

Stacey approached Emerson with a watchful eye on Cailean. She grabbed his fat, stubby finger and pulled on it. "Come on, Daddy, let's go. She's over there and I think I have to go now."

Emerson raised an eyebrow and turned away with a smirk. "If you're hanging around a little while longer, I'll be back in a few minutes."

"Sure," she said and watched him bend oddly as he kept his daughter's hand. He walked to the woman who was waiting. She wore a suit skirt and had a big smile.

"She's fake," Cailean said. "Probably after his money."

She was a slender woman and had a nice tan. The outfit she wore revealed her shapely body and her long, jet-black hair rode the soft breeze.

Cailean took the opportunity to drink some more. Plenty of small sips numbed her throat and she saw Emerson pull something out of his pocket and hand it to the woman. She presumed it was money, and a moment later, he walked away from her.

As Emerson walked back to Cailean, Stacey ran into the playground and the woman with the black hair answered her phone and started taking notes.

"Peculiar," she whispered. "Is that her mother?"

Emerson shook his head. "No, that's Doctor Lee. She cares for my daughter."

Cailean looked at Stacey curiously. There didn't appear to be anything wrong with her.

"It's a long story," he said.

"We all have at least one of those, don't we?"

He nodded. "Well, I'm going to be here next week. It can be right around the same time if you want to get the kids together."

"I'm married," she said.

He smiled. "I know. I saw your ring. I'm just looking for a friend. Lord knows I can use one."

She nodded.

"Me too. Six years I've been married and I've wanted to leave my husband every day since then. There's nothing there. I don't think there ever was anything there. There's no love, communication, or attraction. I swear, I married him to escape a horrible home life and I think that was a bigger mistake. It's like we're roommates and we can't even get along as that."

Emerson nodded.

"I'm sorry," she said. "I just met you and I'm telling you all of this. I'm embarrassed."

"Don't be," he said.

"Are you married?"

"No, not anymore. My wife died some years back."

"I'm sorry."

"Yeah, me too," he said. "That's why Stacey has been under the guidance of a doctor. She witnessed something horrible and I'm not quite sure how it has affected her."

"That sounds tragic," Cailean said, and motioned towards Beau. "He's the only reason I stick around."

He shook his head and sat next to her on the bench. She capped the water bottle to try and contain the odor.

"It's never a good idea to stay around for the child," he said. "Although your intentions are good, you're going to do more harm than good if you fight in front of him."

She smiled, crossed her legs, and leaned towards him with her best smile. "You're very smart."

"Maybe we can talk some more about the things that trouble you. I'm a really good listener and I've learned some lessons about the importance of not keeping everything bottled up inside."

She smiled. "Sure, that would be nice."

"OK," he said and took his car keys out of his pocket. The gold Jaguar pendant verified her assumption. Although she remained calm on the outside, on the inside joy overtook her. She felt like she'd just hit the lottery.

"Well, next week it is then," he said. "I'll send you the picture of you and your son. Maybe I'll leave it as a surprise."

He turned around and walked away, but this time, she watched the water. The wind gently caressed her and rippled the surface of the river.

"Beau, five minutes!" Cailean said, feeling fine.

A swell of emotion filled with the possibility that Emerson may very well be her ticket out of her lousy marriage relaxed her. She was more than willing to give him back whatever he desired, no matter how repulsed she might be while doing it.

Panic-stricken screams erupted and she jumped. The sheer terror in them made the skin on her arms goose. She stood and searched the park for the reason behind the sudden panic. People ran past her, moving towards the far corner of the playground. The colossal structure blocked her view, but with all of the commotion this had to be something awful. She walked towards the gathering. Gasps, mumbled chatter, and horrified expressions aroused her curiosity and she needed to see what the fuss was about.

Wiggling her way through the tight crowd, she stopped when she saw Beau sprawled on the ground with his hips twisted in such a way that she knew it was bad.

"Beau!"

She lunged forward to grab him. She intended on pulling him to his feet, brushing off his clothes, and scolding him for scaring her so. But powerful hands clamped down on her shoulders and kept her away from her son.

"Beau, get up!" she shouted. She turned and punched the person who held her. "Get your damn hands off of me!"

"No. Don't touch him. He can't be moved."

"But that's my son," she shouted. Rafi was lying on the ground next to him, just out of reach. "I can't just leave him there like that. I need to help him."

"You'll help him more by not moving him."

"No!" she said and tried to fight against his incredible strength.

"Look at me." Hands grabbed her face and forced her focus. Emerson's stare was intense. "You cannot move him, do you understand me?"

Her fight went away and her eyes filled with tears.

"Here," he said, and took the water bottle out of her hand. "Let's get you some more water." He hesitated, brought the bottle to his nose and sniffed it.

She ripped the bottle from his hand. "You keep your mouth shut. This is none of your business."

"No, it's not," he said and pointed at the park facility building. "Go to the water fountain and refill your bottle." He handed her gum he pulled from his pocket. "I'll look after your son while you get yourself together."

She kept her shame hidden behind the tint of her glasses. Stepping past Emerson, she concentrated on walking a straight line to the fountain.

19

WHAT'S INSIDE

Present day.

Cailean sat at the table and noticed Rafi remained in her firm grasp.

"The things you do, the way you are, it's because of what resides in you," Sariel said.

Her heart was heavy from the events she just experienced. Having her suspicion validated that she was indeed responsible for Beau being in a wheelchair brought her to her breaking point.

"I don't care anymore," she said. "There is nothing left for us to talk about. I will never be able to move past that event in death, as I wasn't able to in life. It's impossible."

"The time has come for us to confront it and it knows," he said.

An intense restlessness came over her and the rousing had become so powerful that it made her feel sick.

"Orthon," Sariel said. "I know you are in there. Your hold on her must come to an end now."

"Help me," Cailean said, though she didn't know why. She found herself in a struggle with something on the inside. The compulsive urge that she should leave the light right now—that this might be her last chance to escape before a strict, unmerciful punishment was handed down—made her desperate and she looked for a way out.

"Cailean?"

It was hard to focus, but she looked at the darkness.

"You will not survive one moment outside the light," Sariel said. "Resist what it is telling you to do."

A shimmer around Sariel flashed and faded. Cailean comprehended that he had sent a message without words. She trusted him and gave up her fight.

"I wish to speak to Orthon. Alone," he said.

Cailean trembled.

"Orthon?"

"Death," Cailean said, but in a voice far more gruesome than Sariel's.

"So, you have come?" Sariel said.

"You beckon me by name when you have no authority over my kind?"

"The authority to bring death to all things living is mine and mine alone. I have the ability to bring an end to your kind, too," he said. "Look around you, you have nowhere to go and you are at my mercy."

"I know no mercy."

Sariel laughed. "Neither will she once you come out and show her what you look like."

Sariel's words had agitated the thing inside her and it relinquished control back to Cailean. She bent at the waist, grabbed her abdomen, and fell to her knees. Fighting what felt like a tug of war on her insides, a cavernous, pain-filled groan was interrupted by a diabolical laughter that sounded inhuman. Orthon had regained control over Cailean.

"Your laughter is how you express fear," Sariel said. "You are vile and weak and you know that you have made a terrible error in coming here today, to my domain."

It lowered her chin and gobs of drool spilled out of her mouth. A menacing, territorial growl warned of the contained aggression and it watched the darkness with wide, unblinking eyes.

"The noises you make are as pathetic as your idea to think you could hide in there and that I wouldn't notice," Sariel said.

"I won't leave her body until she has departed from the living world. You have taken her here prematurely and I still have claim over her. I will tell her of your plan unless you leave me be."

"If you knew what I planned, demon, then you would not have come here now. You are nothing but the dirt beneath everyone's feet. You feed off of the young and weary and make their lives miserable. I see no use for your kind. Now, come forth so she can see you for what you are."

It attempted to smile. "No, I told you that she is mine until this body dies."

"I can take her now and you with her. Maybe I will send you for judgment, too. Imagine what would happen."

The smile disappeared and the low raspy growl returned.

"Release her of your control and I may have mercy on you."

At that command, Cailean's body went limp and collapsed on the floor face first. A split second later, she arched back and teetered on her stomach. Her voice strained with a scream forced out by pure pain and her eyes bulged. Veins inside her eyes burst and her scleras turned red.

Like a puppet controlled by a puppeteer, she rose up, stood, and tilted her head back. Her mouth opened fully and she made a monstrous retching sound. Long, charred fingers reached out of her mouth and grabbed her upper and lower jaws and pried them apart.

She leaned forward and something abhorrent spilled from her mouth. It hurried to its feet and stood in a large pool of vomit. It had a skinless face. Sharp, menacing teeth snapped at the air, and red eyes smoldering like hot coals stared back at her.

She turned away from it, frightened and repulsed.

"Fear it no more," Sariel said. "It knows it can no longer hurt you. It feels trapped like a wild animal and it knows it will be put down."

Orthon belted out a ferocious growl and Cailean sidestepped it.

"I don't like it," she said, her eyes wide with fear.

"Two chairs," Sariel said. "Place them close and face them. This is your chance to confront it."

An unseen nudge encouraged Cailean's feet into motion. She gathered the chairs and positioned them a few feet apart, unnerved by the close quarters.

"You belong to me!" Orthon said, and shoved the chair aside. It tumbled across the floor and the loud sounds startled Cailean. "You side with that thing out there?" It pointed at the darkness. "Look at all of the things I have given you."

Sariel laughed and Cailean clamped her eyes shut.

"I don't like this!" she shouted.

"I want you to look at it!" Sariel said.

She opened her eyes to see the thing that stood before her and gasped. Sexless and naked it stood about five feet tall. Its body was fat and charcoal colored flesh was cracked and peeling. The arms and legs were different lengths and chewed meat clung to its sharp teeth.

"What do you see?" Sariel said.

She remembered the pain within her belly and the constant unquenchable thirst. She saw that the meat in its teeth was the lies and anger she fed it. Her face twisted into an expression of revulsion. "I see pure evil."

"What you see standing before you now was much smaller and weaker when you were a child. But you chose to embrace it and nurture it, and it has lived and grown inside of you. This is what has encouraged you to make the decisions you have made."

It didn't blink and it gave off a foul odor that reminded her of Mr. Hagen. She wondered if he was infected that day in the lily field and had somehow passed it to her.

"Daddy," Orthon said, its lurid voice scorned Cailean.

"Stop it!" she said.

"He loved you but you loved me more."

Now it mocked her.

The hairs on the back of her neck stood up and the shame and anger that battled within distracted her.

"And your mommy?" Orthon said.

"Shut up," she said.

"I needed them out of the way," Orthon said and tilted its head. "A suggestion here and there led to that very important lie. One that would allow me to get a hold of you and remove anything positive that influenced you."

"Why?"

"Because you hated the man across the street. Hate and misery are what I feed off of. And because of you, I have eaten well."

Cailean forbade the thought that what she saw before her now had lived inside of her since she was a girl.

"That little girl at the playground with your son is mine after I'm done with you."

"What girl at the playground?"

"The girl and the fat father. What you didn't see was a push and no fall. It was all a lie and I saw it with my own eyes."

It cackled in delight.

"Don't let it distract you. Tell it what you think of it," Sariel said.

Her mind raced with the events Sariel had shared with her.

"Oh yes, have a hard look. You've fed me well," Orthon said with its horrible discordant voice. It banged on its fattened belly with a wet slap. "And there are so many more like you."

The personal torment she suffered at the hands of that thing and the insufferable hurt she put others through because of it brought out a feeling of raw discontent she had never known before and her humanity slipped away in an instant.

"I hate you!" she screamed and the veins in her neck bulged. Clenched fists were ready to lash out and spit flew from her mouth. She stood and went nose to nose with it and shoved it.

"What did you do to me?"

Orthon roared back and tried to grab her but his gooey skin gave him no traction.

"I gave you a purpose!" it said.

She shoved it again and it fell near the edge of light. Panicked, it tried to run away but Sariel grabbed it by its neck and picked it up. Flailing limbs and a hysterical scream came to an end in a fast, brutal flaying by Sariel's fingernails.

He dropped the mangled piece of meat to the ground and the wind kicked up, covering the body with snow.

Dumbfounded, Cailean looked at the spot where it had fallen, but all traces of it were gone.

20

TIME TO STOP

The past.

"You said he has Rafi?"

"Yes," Emerson said and drove his Jaguar hard.

"Are you sure?"

"Yes, I'm sure. I placed it beside him after they strapped him in the stretcher."

He kept pace with the ambulance that rushed Beau to the hospital.

"OK," Cailean said and tried to relax. The quiet growl of the engine hinted at its hidden power and the sleek interior was a great distraction.

"I saw the entire thing," he said. His fat fingers and bloated palms wrapped the steering wheel.

Cailean's heart thundered and she really didn't want to know the particulars. In fact, she didn't want to go to the hospital with Beau, but she couldn't get herself to say so.

"I tried to help him, but I couldn't," he said. "I was too far away, and by the time I even reacted it was all over."

Emerson's focus remained on the road. The ambulance did most of the work clearing a path, and he did an excellent job of keeping up.

"He dropped his giraffe off of the top of the playground and he tried to catch it. He did everything he could not to let it fall." He shook his head. "How could he not sense the danger he was in?"

The image of what happened next was clear in Cailean's mind and a chill coursed through her body. She shifted in her seat, uncomfortable with what she was about to hear next.

"He fell from the side where the cutout is—the side where they have that firehouse pole."

"Oh my God," Cailean said and the sensation of falling overcame her. She shivered, sat up fast, and grabbed the dashboard. A few times in the past she had walked the massive playground structure and felt dizzy by the height and wanted to get down.

"He landed on his head," he said. "And I don't like the way his neck bent when he hit the ground."

A tingle of disgust turned her stomach. She wanted to get out of the car and go somewhere far away. Desperate to separate herself from this moment so she wouldn't have to face it she pulled on the door handle, but it was locked.

"What are you doing?" Emerson said.

"I don't know. I'm freaking out right now and I don't feel well."

"I need you to try and calm down and put your seatbelt on."

"Please stop," she said, and strapped herself in. "I don't want to hear any more." Her pale face was coated with sweat and an obvious tremble coursed through her body.

"OK," he said and glanced at her. "I'm sorry; I shouldn't have told you those things. I guess I'm kinda freaked out, too."

"I should be in that ambulance with him."

"No, you shouldn't. Clearly you are shaken and you need to let them do their work so your son can have the best chance possible."

She turned her head quickly. "Best chance at what? What are you saying?"

Emerson opened his hands and his lips moved without speaking.

"What I'm trying to say is that if you let them work he'll have a better chance at a full recovery."

Cailean stared out the passenger window; like the day, everything went by in a blur.

"You should call your husband and let him know what happened."

She shook her head. "No, I can't. We don't even know what is wrong with Beau yet."

"You're not thinking clearly," he said, his tone firm. "You need to call him now. No matter what he's done wrong, he deserves to know his child is in distress."

"OK," she said, and took her cell phone out of her pocket. Her hand shook uncontrollably and she couldn't operate the touchscreen properly to dial out.

"Damn it!" she shouted in a sudden burst of anger and tossed the phone down by her feet and started to cry.

The ambulance had gained more than a full block on them and the traffic light ahead turned red. The cross traffic started moving and the Jaguar eased to a fast stop.

"Damn," Emerson said and pounded the steering wheel.

"It doesn't matter. I need you to pull over anyway," she said.

"What?" He looked at her.

"Pull over, now!"

Emerson pulled to the side of the road, and before he could bring the vehicle to a complete stop, Cailean flung the door open and ran to the tree line. She vomited several times, her heave louder than the sounds of the passing traffic.

Returning to the vehicle with an overpowering smell of vomit that followed her like a generous spray of bad perfume, she spit on the ground and wiped her mouth with the back of her hand.

"I need you to take me to a convenience store," she said.

"But what about your son? We have to get to the hospital." He pointed in the direction the ambulance drove off in. "They're way ahead of us."

She wiped her mouth with her sleeve. "He wasn't even conscious when they took him. He wouldn't know if I was there or not. My stomach is in knots and I have a feeling that this is going to be the longest day of my life. I need to get this taste out of my mouth."

"OK."

She sat in the car and buckled herself in. "Thank you."

"Are you OK?"

"I'm trying to figure that out."

"It's OK, I'm here for you," he said.

"I don't think I can face him."

"You have to. He's your son."

"I know, but this all happened because I wasn't paying attention. I was too busy talking to you . . . and drinking."

"It was an accident."

"Would you consider going into the hospital with me? I don't want to have to do this alone."

Emerson shook his head. "I don't want to overstep my bounds. I think this is a private matter for you and your husband."

"Please," she said. "It would help me a great deal if you were there. You don't have to say or do anything. Just be there."

He gave in with a nod. "OK, but at least call your husband and tell him what happened."

He handed her his phone.

"I can't thank you enough," she said. "I don't know why you're being so nice to me, but I appreciate it more than I could ever say."

"It's the least I can do."

She took the phone from him and dialed Wilson's phone number with the tremble still shaking her hands. Turning her back to Emerson, she placed the phone against her ear and dreaded having to hear the sound of Wilson's voice.

Cailean stood outside of the Jaguar on the driver's side. Emerson rolled down the window and waited for Cailean to speak.

"I need to use the restroom, too, while I'm here. I'm going to wash up and it is going to take me a few extra minutes. Do you need me to bring you out anything?"

"No," Emerson said. "But thank you. I need to use the time to call Stacey's doctor and see how she is."

She acknowledged what he said with a subtle nod. "I shouldn't be too long."

She walked into the 7-11. The beverage aisle ran along the side and rear wall of the store and the snack aisle was located directly across from that. The solid wall of aluminum, plastic, and glass bottles was stocked full and displayed behind glass doors that kept them cold. The order of selection went from sports drinks, water, soda, and lastly, beer.

She pretended to browse the snacks so she could have a look at Emerson over the four-foot high aisles. His attention remained away from the store and his cell phone was pressed firmly against his ear. While he spoke, his free hand waved around and seemed to follow each word.

Cailean moved fast. She pulled the refrigerator door open, grabbed a twelve-pack, and hurried to the register.

"I need to use the restroom," she said and glanced over her shoulder to see if Emerson was still occupied. Satisfied that he was, she paid the cashier with crumpled bills that were stuffed in the pockets of her jacket and she hurried to the bathroom with her purchase.

Ignoring the handwritten *No merchandise in bathroom!* sign, she entered the small room that reeked of cleaning products. A toilet bowl, sink with no counter, metal garbage can, hazy mirror, and a wall mounted electric powered hand dryer were the only fixtures in the room. Locking the door, she placed the cardboard case into the sink and shook in anticipation.

The crack of the pull-tab splitting the perforated aluminum caused her to moan in anticipation. Cold vapor oozed from the hole like a curled finger inviting her in. Titling her head back, she gulped down the beer and stopped only when the can completely emptied. A series of burps made enough room in her gut for the next beer.

She tossed the empty can into the trash and quickly opened another. As she drank each one, regret began to settle in and interrupt her rhythm—maybe she should have gotten a full case instead of a twelve pack.

"Are you sure you think this is a good idea?" Emerson said.

Cailean mustered the most convincing tone she could and looked at Emerson. "I've never been so certain in my life until now."

"Your speech is slurred, you can barely keep your eyes open, and you smell like you've bathed in beer."

"Well what the hell do you expect?" she said, and shook her head and folded her arms across her chest. "Look at what I'm going through! I just needed a little something to help me with my nerves. I'm fine."

The elevator slowed and lurched to a stop. She stumbled and teetered and Emerson caught her.

"Easy," he said, and held her upright.

"No, that wasn't my fault," she said and worked on finding her balance. "I wasn't expecting the elevator to jerk like that."

"Listen, I really don't want to get in the middle of this. I'll make sure you get to your son, and then I'm going to leave. I'm sure your husband is here by now and you two will need to talk."

"Screw him. I don't have anything to say to him."

"For your son's sake you two need to open up the lines of communication. You're stronger working together than apart. Believe me, I know."

"What are you talking about?"

"The dysfunction and how it affected the people close to me."

"It seems to me you have a lot of money and yet you're talking to me about dysfunction?" She laughed. "Something about what you're saying doesn't make much sense."

"It's not funny," he said.

"I wish I had your problem."

"No, you don't. And believe me, money doesn't fix everything."

"No, but it sure would help."

"I would give away everything I have to make my problems disappear."

They stepped into the quiet lobby with only one direction to go in. Heavy double doors blocked the way.

"Well, it doesn't matter how hard I try," she said. "Wilson will never understand me. He's an idiot and I can guarantee you that he's going to give me all sorts of hell over this."

"That's why I told you I felt this was a private time for your family."

Emerson pulled the door open and it moved with ease.

"If you want to leave me, then go ahead. I thought we were becoming friends, but I see you're a phony just like everyone else. Get back into your fancy car and drive away. Just forget about my problems and me. I handled my business before you came and I can handle it after you're gone."

"Listen," he said. "I didn't mean it to sound like I was leaving you or forgetting you forever. I would like to know how your son is and I want to be your friend. This is just something I feel I shouldn't be in the middle of."

"How could you say that?" She stared at him with bright red eyes that begged him for support. "You were there. You saw the entire thing and you helped him. You are a part of this!"

"No, I'm not. Not the way I ever wanted to be."

"If it weren't for you I might've moved him and injured him further."

"Yeah, if it wasn't for me . . . I feel guilty about it, too. If we never met this wouldn't have happened. If I was standing a little closer I might have caught him before he hit the ground and we'd be laughing instead of doing this."

"You know what? Why don't you just forget it. Thank you for everything you've done," she said, and turned away from him and fell. Emerson rushed to her side and helped her stand.

"You won't make it ten feet alone in your condition."

"I guess I am that drunk."

"Come on, I'll take you."

The white walls, bright lights, and polished floor made Cailean squint.

"What room did they say he was in?" she said.

"Number six."

She tittered. "A place this big and they put him in room six?"

Her voice echoed and the slur in her words was obvious.

"Try and keep your voice down," Emerson said. "We're in a hospital, not a nightclub."

He encouraged her to continue walking the long, empty hall with a tug on her jacket. The rooms started at number thirty and counted downwards.

"We have to walk down to the end," he said.

"All the way down there?" Cailean stopped and pointed.

"Are you going to be able to make it down there?"

Her expression went from doubt to acceptance in a matter of moments. "I can do that, no problem."

"Let's go then, and quit stopping so much."

She saluted him and walked the hallway.

"Tell me you noticed that the little bastard couldn't make it easy on me by getting a room closer to the elevator."

"You shouldn't say things like that."

"Why not?" she said. "I've gotta walk all the way to the end."

"Because people might take you seriously."

"But I am being serious. You might not know this, but Beau has always given me trouble."

Emerson sighed. "I think you've had way too much to drink. You're saying these things because you're upset and drunk. Now let's get to your son. We don't want to keep him waiting any longer than we already have."

"No, wait," she said and stood her ground. "I need to ask you something first."

"What is it?"

"Do you think Beau might have done this on purpose?"

He gave her a double take. "Done what on purpose?"

"Fall."

"Fall?"

"Yes, fall. Do you think he did it to get attention?"

"Are you serious?" Emerson shook his head. "I can't believe you're even saying that. I told you I saw the entire thing and it wasn't on purpose."

He looked up and down the corridor and saw that they were alone.

"And I said that I think you should be careful with the things you say. Growing up my father always told me that what is in a drunk person's words is what is in their sober heart."

"And my daddy was a killer. Do you know what he told me?"

Emerson didn't respond.

"He told me that I didn't have to worry about anyone hurting me ever again. He was full of crap."

"Stop and listen to what you're saying."

"Don't tell me what to do."

"Come on," he said and tugged on her jacket again.

"Stop pulling on me," she said, and pulled back. "I can't stand that."

"Well, I need you to keep moving. You said you could do this, that it was no problem."

"I can. But you don't need to yank on my damn jacket."

They neared the end of the hallway without further incident. The last door was number fifteen and the hallway bent to the right. A small black sign mounted on the wall directed them to rooms fourteen down to one.

"We have to go this way," he said and continued on.

"No!" she said and plopped herself down on the floor. "Where are you taking me? Where is my son? And does Wilson have something to do with this?"

"Your son is at the end of this hall. Come on."

"Are you trying to keep me from seeing him or something? Is this some sort of sick joke?"

"No, it's not," he said and looked down both corridors. Members of the medical staff had emerged from their rooms and were watching them.

"Keep your voice down," he said. "I didn't know there was another hallway and you're being really loud."

"I don't care."

"I do," he said and knelt beside her. "I'm trying to help you like you've asked."

"Then tell me why are the rooms spaced so far apart?"

"I don't know, but we need to move on. We're starting to get everyone's attention and not in a good way."

She looked left and right and indignation curled her lips. "What are you people looking at? My son is probably going to die and you're all judging me because I'm upset? Give me a break!"

Emerson stood. "Come on, Cailean, let's go."

"Screw them! Every single one of them!"

"Your son needs you. Don't get yourself thrown out of here."

She snickered. "I'd like to see them try and keep him from me."

"Cailean, we need to go."

"They're all lucky you decided to come with me or I'd turn this place upside down."

"Did you hear what I said? Now is not the time for this. Your son needs you."

"And how the hell do you know what he needs? I want to know, are you a doctor or something?"

"No, I'm not. I'm a struggling father with a boatload of my own problems. But I saw your son fall and I saw how bad it was."

"Yeah, well," she whispered. "I just fell and I'm fine."

"You sat down. I assure you that you didn't fall like he did."

The hallways cleared of the people.

"Why are you even here?" she said.

"I'm here because you asked me," he said. "You told me you needed me here and I sympathized."

"Maybe one day we can talk about the problems you say you have and we'll see how they compare to mine," she said. "I'll bet you they don't even come close to the things I've gone through."

Reproachable thoughts filled her head and threatened to come out, but then she remembered: this big, fat, ugly man with his pockmarked face and constant sweat was the perfect crutch for her. It was obvious she could manipulate him in anyway she wanted and that was exactly what she needed.

"I've been crapped on since I was a kid," she said.

"I'm sorry."

She waved a dismissive hand. "Ah, what does it matter? It's really not your problem."

She stood, neatened her clothing and recounted all the things he had done for her so far. He had seen her at her worst and yet here he was, still by her side.

"I can only imagine what your story is," she said.

"I think it's like you said. It pales in comparison to yours."

She smiled as if that admission was somehow an advantage.

"Maybe I should have gotten him some flowers or something," she said.

Wilson emerged from the room, rigid and pale. His eyes were like two glowing taillights and his sullen expression looked as though it had been carved from a slab of granite.

"He's in a coma," he said, his composure fragile.

Those words stopped her cold and diluted her buzz.

"They said he has a broken neck and they're going to need to operate on him once the swelling goes down. The doctor told me there is a possibility he may never walk again. They really don't know. They're saying it's too soon to tell, but they want to prepare us for the worst."

"No," she said and shook her head hysterically. "He only fell. He always gets up after he falls."

Tears leaked from Wilson's reddened eyes and he stepped towards her with his arms extended, looking to hold her.

"No!" she shouted, and turned her back on Wilson. She reached for Emerson. "I don't want you near me."

Wilson stopped and sniffed the air. The granite look of despair fell away and was replaced with discontent. "You've been drinking again, Cailean, I can smell it from here."

"What difference does that make?"

She hid her face.

"Our son needs you—I need you, and this is how you come here?"

"He's not even awake, Wilson. He doesn't know whether I'm here or not. So what does it matter if I stopped and had a few beers? You know how my nerves are."

"You're irresponsible and insensitive to the people around you, Cailean!"

"And you're a judgmental passive aggressive shit and I've had it with you."

"Why did you make him ride in the ambulance alone?"

"I wanted to make sure I wasn't in their way!"

"Why didn't you give him Rafi? You know that is the only thing that comforts him."

"It was sent along with him in the ambulance."

Wilson shook his head. "No it wasn't. They said he didn't arrive with anyone or anything. We should have that for him when he wakes. He'll be asking for him."

"They're lying! They've lost it!" she said, her face twisted and grotesque. She looked at Emerson. "It was sent on the ambulance with him, isn't that what you said?"

"Yes, I made sure of it."

"You see?"

"Who is he?" Wilson said.

"He is none of your damn business, that's who he is."

Wilson eyed Emerson. "Who are you and what are you doing here with my wife? This is a private matter."

She grabbed Emerson's hand. "You don't have to answer him!" She looked at Wilson. "What does it matter to you anyway? You don't give a damn about me when I'm around."

"Because you're like this all too often. I suppose it doesn't matter," Wilson said. "I guess it hasn't mattered for a long time now."

"Ma'am?"

Cailean looked at a faceless nurse.

"We allowed you your outburst earlier, but now we're going to have to ask you to lower your voice and conduct yourself properly or I'm going to have to ask you to leave."

Cailean scowled. "How dare you be so cold to me? My son has been in a terrible accident and this is the way you treat his grieving parent?"

"I understand—"

"You understand? You think you do because you've been trained to deal with tragedy while you wear a plastic smile, but you don't! You probably don't even have children."

"Cailean, that's enough," Wilson said.

"Screw off, Wilson!"

"Come on," Emerson said and led her away by the hand. "Come with me. Let me get you out of here so you can cool down."

"Gladly," she said. "You should be thanking this man, Wilson; not accusing him of any wrongdoing. He was the man that went to Beau's side when he fell from the playground."

"He is?"

"Yes, he is!"

Wilson swallowed hard. "I'm sorry, mister, I didn't know. I'm not thinking right. Thank you for helping my son."

"You owe him more than that," she said and walked away.

21

MY ANGEL DIED

Present day.

Rafi looked back at Cailean from her numb hand, worn and sad. But it had a relentless stare that challenged her distaste for him when all he did was comfort her son in his time of need.

"I'm sorry," she said, but it continued to watch her and work on her defenses.

"If you could speak, I'm sure you would have plenty to say to me," she said.

The realization that a stuffed animal had been a better parent than she had been nearly brought her to tears.

"I don't know what else to say to you," she said, as the smell that emanated from it got stronger and sickened her. A look of displeasure took over her face and she held Rafi away.

"What do you expect?" Sariel said.

She lowered Rafi by her side and waited for him to finish his point.

"When you don't care for something it withers. And the thing you are holding is merely made of cotton." He sighed. "Imagine how spoiled things are on the inside of Beau after all the longing and desire to be loved has gone unfulfilled."

She opposed the thought and brought Rafi to her nose and squeezed him, searching for something specific. Drawing a deep breath, she searched for the slightest hint of Beau's scent. Dirty water oozed from his body and with it, an indescribable smell of wet, rancid decay filled her nostrils and made her gag.

"There is nothing left of him in there," he said. "It has been spoiled by your self-regard and poor parenting skills."

"I didn't know what I was doing. That thing inside of me made me do things I wouldn't have normally done."

Laughter that was light and genuine echoed all around her. Rafi fell out of her hand and landed in the snow with a weighty plop.

"How could you laugh at such a horrible thing?"

She waited for an explanation but none was offered.

"I saw what it was and it was vile—evil personified—and I can't believe it lived inside of me. My skin is crawling and I still feel sick to my stomach over what I have seen here."

"I laughed because you chose to embrace it. Even as you slipped further and further into moral corruption, something else inside screamed for your attention. It told you that what you were doing was wrong. But you chose to ignore her. You always decided to listen after it was too late."

Faint crying interrupted their conversation. She turned and listened. Strangely, the sound came from within the light and its location was very specific.

Crouching and looking beneath the table, she saw a little girl curled in the fetal position, whimpering and mumbling incoherently.

"Are you OK?" Cailean said, and everything else was immediately replaced by her concern for her.

Thin and weak, the child could barely lift her head. Sunken eyes that carried a profound sadness were difficult to look at. They told of horrible abuse and the absence of any self-worth. It broke Cailean's heart to see her like this and she needed to offer her assistance.

"Who is this and why is she like this?" Cailean said.

"You don't recognize her?"

Unkempt hair hid most of her face, and Cailean sat and looked at the pall where Sariel had killed the imp. "No, I don't know her," she said.

"Has it really been that long for you?"

Cailean turned her attention back to the girl. Moving with caution, she went to brush the hair out of her eyes but the little girl flinched and tried to move away.

"It's OK, I won't hurt you," she said gently.

The girl watched Cailean with fear and distrust.

"I won't hurt you," she said again.

"But you already have," Sariel said.

The young girl submitted to Cailean's touch. She brushed her hair aside.

Cailean gasped.

"Yes," Sariel said. "She's the cute little girl with the freckles. This was you as a child."

"What happened to her?"

"She hasn't seen anything but the demon," Sariel said. "She was trapped inside of you with it, suffering its torment, unable to grow or escape its wrath since you chose to embrace it."

The thought of having to allow the demon to mature while she endured such abuse for so long compelled Cailean to reach her hand out in a willing gesture to offer comfort.

"I am so sorry," she said, unsure of what else she could say or do to change this.

"She is the one who tried to gain your attention, but you chose to ignore her," he said. "Your angel inside has paid the ultimate price. She's been devoured by your demon."

The child extended a frail, trembling hand to meet Cailean's in an expression of acceptance. Through the numbness that consumed Cailean, she could feel the cold that gripped the little girl.

Gently, she extracted the girl out from underneath the table. Her frail, skeletal frame barely weighed anything.

"You're OK now," Cailean said, and the little girl moaned and tried to shield her eyes from the bright overhead light. But she didn't have the strength to hold her hand up.

"That is what is left of the goodness within you," he said. "Starved of all attention and left to die because you chose to feed the wicked thing instead."

"I will nurture her and bring her back to health," Cailean said, and stroked her long auburn hair. "I can change."

"No, it is too late for her now."

"Just give me one more chance before you take her, please!"

The little girl choked and convulsed. Frightened, Cailean pulled her close and held her tight.

"Your decisions have killed her," he said. "And you are left with nothing but the reality of your cruelness and the regret that has now come to fill those voids."

An unseen force came like a strong blow of air and took the body away. Cailean stared at her empty hands and cried for all the things she had lost in her life.

22

I CHOOSE THE BOTTLE

The past.

Cailean leaned on the counter and twirled the near empty bottle of wine in her hands. She listened to the liquid slosh around and watched the label appear, disappear, and reappear again as it went around and around.

You're in over your head.

"Mom, you told me to remind you when I needed to go to the bathroom and I don't know if you're hearing me!" Beau shouted from the television room.

How can you just stand there and listen to that?

"Mommy?"

She gritted her teeth and whispered, "This kid does not give up."

You can bend so far before you break.

"Mom, can you hear me calling you?"

She took another drink.

"Mom!"

Her composure broke.

I told you.

"Beau, shut your mouth! You've called my name a hundred times. How do you think it is even possible I didn't hear you?"

"I'm sorry, Mom, I don't want to have an accident."

She sighed.

"Just give me a minute, will you!"

You know he's going to keep pushing.

"Can't you come now?" he said.

I told you.

An unpredictable surge of anger made her slam the bottle down.

"I hope you crap yourself," she shouted. "Maybe you'd give up this pointless fight of not trying to dirty yourself."

The ordeal of having to lift Beau out of his chair, onto the floor, and then back into his chair again infuriated her. Wilson allowed Beau to do whatever he pleased because he felt bad for him and it had turned him into this demanding spoiled brat that she really wasn't fond of.

"What have I gotten myself into?"

A horrible situation I see no way out of.

"I shouldn't have believed I could do this."

Wilson set you up for failure.

"How so?"

He's the one who kept you away from Beau for so long. No wonder you've forgotten the basic skills you need to make this successful.

"You got me good this time, Wilson," she said.

Something within gave her the idea that this was becoming a dangerous situation for Beau. It encouraged her to pick up the phone and to call Wilson and admit that she was unfit to do this. But a strong contradicting feeling inserted itself firmly into place and took over completely. It was the one that defied the idea of admitting anything to Wilson and it disallowed her to show weakness.

"It's not a big deal, Mom," Beau said. "If you want, I can go myself and if I have any trouble, I'll call you."

"Get that out of your head, Beau. I'm not even going to entertain the thought of allowing you to go in there without me being near," she said. "I'm coming right now so get off of my back. I don't want anything happening to you."

"Nothing is going to happen."

"You don't know that."

She firmed her balance and plotted her course back to Beau.

"Idiotic kid thinks he knows it all."

She stumbled and held onto things for balance as she walked out of the kitchen.

"Why can't you get it through that thick head of yours that the last thing I need you to do is fall again? God forbid if you were to get hurt even worse than you did before. Your father is difficult enough without my having to hear him use every opportunity to tell me how bad my parenting skills are."

"I haven't fallen since the accident."

"Was it my imagination or did you not fall in the bathroom before?"

"I slipped."

"You fell."

"I really need to go to the bathroom."

She bumped the wall and staggered.

"Yeah, yeah, yeah. Why don't you wait until the last second to tell me next time?"

"But I've been calling for you for a long time."

She entered the living room and Beau watched her with angry eyes.

"What? Why are you looking at me like that?" she said.

"I'm not looking at you like anything, Mom. I've been waiting here longer than I should and I don't want to have an accident."

"You sound like a broken record, you know that? I want you to know that it's driving me nuts." She settled behind the wheelchair and disengaged the brakes.

"I'm sorry if I'm bothering you," he said. "You told me to remind you and I wasn't sure if you heard me. I thought you were just ignoring me for some reason."

"First, there's a big difference between reminding and whining. Second, when you whine like that I really don't want to be around you. Why don't you wear a damn diaper if you're so worried about crapping yourself?"

"I do wear a diaper. But Dad says I have to keep it on just in case of an accident."

She stared at the back of his head, loathing him. He just sat there, as useless as his legs.

"I couldn't care less about what your father tells you. Don't you think if you just went in your diaper that it would have made our time a lot less stressful? This constant back and forth to the bathroom is tiresome."

"I'm not a baby anymore, Mom. I need to go to the bathroom like all the other kids my age do."

"And it doesn't matter to you how much it puts the people around you out, does it?" She shook her head. "Get it through your head that you're not like the other kids because they're not confined to a wheelchair like you!"

His body trembled and he cried quietly.

"I know I'm not," he said. "And you're not like other mothers."

Cailean stepped beside Beau and moved close to him. "What did you just say?"

"Nothing."

"I want you to tell me what you said and I want you to say it to my face."

Beau stared at her with bright red eyes, unable to speak.

"You're a coward, do you know that? You're just like your father."

She moved beside him again and thought about smacking him in the head, but the scar the surgery had left on his neck reasoned with her.

"Don't talk about my dad," he said. "He's good to me."

"You mumble stuff underneath your breath so I can't hear it. And when I give you the perfect opportunity to tell me what's on your mind, you start to cry and chicken out."

She gave the wheelchair a strong push and the handrim on the wheel got hung up on the coffee table and dragged it along. Cailean pushed harder to try and dislodge it, but the table skidded across the floor, bunched the area rug and turned the wheelchair askew, stopping it.

"Damn it!" Cailean said and fell down with a heavy thump.

"Mom?" Beau shifted in his chair. "Are you OK?"

"Don't worry about me," she said and was slow to get up. She kicked the table away with a yell and rubbed what hurt.

"You should have said it, Beau. Maybe if you did I would respect you more despite your stupid fascination of not wanting to piss in your diaper. At least that would have shown me you were becoming a man."

Anger lingered and there were no more words to say. She pushed Beau towards the bathroom.

23

BEAU'S FATE

Present day.

Cailean gasped, jumped back and fell down. She scrambled away and stopped at the veil where the darkness met the light. Pressing her back dangerously close to the biting cold, she stared at Beau with wide, disbelieving eyes.

"What is he doing here?" she said, rigid and inert.

He sat perfectly still at the table with his arms dangling limply by his sides. His mouth hung open and drool dripped into his lap. A deep stare that focused on something hidden within the unnatural backdrop held his attention firmly.

"Beau?" she said and kept her distance while she watched him.

"He cannot hear you," Sariel said.

"What do you mean he can't hear me? He's right there! Beau, please tell me what you're doing here."

Beau didn't react to the sound of her voice, and the genuine concern that came over Cailean was foreign. Like anything else that was good, she didn't know what to do with it.

"Beau, honey," she called to him again, and strangely she was reminded of when he needed to go to the bathroom and she ignored him.

"But that was different," she reasoned, and discarded the thought. "It's Mommy, can you hear me?"

She stood and paused to scrutinize him further. He didn't blink and didn't appear to be breathing. She moved towards him.

"Are you hurt?"

She continued her approach and her worry only deepened the closer she got to him.

"Why isn't he answering me?"

"Death has come upon your son," Sariel said and the words were like a stiff punch to Cailean's gut.

"What?" she said and shook her head. "No, that isn't possible. You've been here with me the entire time."

"A touch is all it takes," he said. "I can move between your thoughts. Those moments are long enough for me to fulfill my obligations."

"Why?" she said, and wept in her hands. All feeling in her skin was gone, and only the pain in her heart remained. "Why him?"

"Yes, Cailean, why him?"

"I don't know," she said, and felt helpless. "I want you to take me instead of him."

"Oh, I *am* going to take you," Sariel said, and the jarring sound of his fingernails rubbing together in anticipation sent a shiver down her spine.

"Please tell me there is hope for him."

"Look at him and tell me what you see. Is he beyond saving?"

He appeared pallid and fragile and it reminded her of her late good side.

"You've brought him here for me to see," she said. "That must mean he is still alive and that must mean there is still hope for him."

"Yes, but if you are to save him you must act quickly."

Free of her demon, the instinct to protect Beau made her run to his side. She went to take his hand into her own and he flinched. His mouth opened wide and formed a perfect circle filled with silent, unspeakable sorrow. Then, a slow, escalating scream reached a deafening level and the strain cracked his young, undeveloped vocal chords and reddened his pale face.

She released him and stared at him, unsure what to do next.

"Please, I don't know what to do and he needs your help," Cailean said to Sariel.

"There is nothing I can do. I have done my part."

Beau continued to scream and Cailean looked at the darkness, and then back at Beau, still unsure what to do.

"Please," she said. "Help my son."

"You are the only one who can help him now."

"Make him stop," she said and covered her ears. "I can't think clearly."

But he continued to wail, uninterrupted, until he ran out of breath. And as if he were completely unaware of what had just happened, he looked forward and assumed the same position she found him in.

"Now is your last chance to prove your love for him," Sariel said.

"I don't know how," she said and beat the tabletop with her numb fists. "I don't know what love is!"

"Dig deep and give him what you have deprived him of for so long."

She continued to watch Beau and he just sat there, devoid of life. And in that instant, the parallel design of Sariel's plan became evident. The opportunity for her to redeem herself had finally come.

Guided by something unknown, she found Rafi in the wet snow and wrung the water out of him. She settled next to Beau and evaluated the stuffed animal one final time. She petted it and could feel her heart filling with a true desire to bring Beau joy.

"I'm sorry for everything I've ever done to you," she said, and placed Rafi in his lap and gently touched his hand. "I am so very sorry, son. I have embraced things in my life I could never hope to understand and I visited that upon you and so many others. And for that I am ashamed. You deserve a life of happiness and now I understand that means I cannot be a part of it. I love you, son."

Beau looked at his mother's touch, and after the briefest pause he busied himself with a slow, unorganized search that ended when his focus settled on Rafi.

"You've come back to me!" he said and scooped up the stuffed animal and lifted it up high. With a bright smile and a look of perfect pleasure, he kissed his friend and hugged him tightly.

Watching the way he loved Rafi filled Cailean with an overpowering feeling of regret. In that moment, she knew that what he had for that inanimate thing could have been hers. But she chose everything that was bad and made a conscious choice to ignore that which was most precious of all.

"I need to know how this happened," she said.

"You will," he said. "And it's like I told you when I first brought you here: you will hate what you were. He isn't as strong as you and the process will consume his body quickly, giving us very little time now."

She knew exactly what Sariel had meant by the process. It was the tingle that started in the hands and feet and crawled deeper into the body every passing second. It was creeping death settling in, and she concluded that once it took over completely, the soul started to separate from the body and there was no chance of ever going back.

24

DEAD WEIGHT

The past.

"Are you done yet?" Cailean said.

"No, not yet," Beau replied.

"This is ridiculous. I don't understand what's taking you so long!"

"I just need one more second, Mom."

She pounded the door. "You're really starting to tick me off."

"OK, you can come in now, I'm done," he said.

She grabbed the doorknob, twisted it, and paused.

"You know something?" she said, and let go of the doorknob. "Now I think you're going to have to wait until I'm ready to help you."

"Mom?"

She stumbled down the hallway in search of the bit of wine she left on the counter. It would help quiet the inner demon that demanded a reprieve from the nonsense she had gotten herself into.

I told you this was a bad idea.

"Mom, where did you go?"

The concern in his voice didn't matter to her. She would get him when she reached a certain level of satisfaction and not a moment before.

"Please, don't leave me here," he said, his voice muffled by the closed door. "I really need to get down, Mom!"

"Shut the hell up," she said, and the effort was weak. Sick and tired, she picked up the bottle and drank until it was empty.

"But, Mom!"

"I swear, this damn kid and his father are going to be the death of me," she said and ripped the refrigerator door open. The second bottle of wine Emerson had brought her sat on the top shelf, front and center. She would need to finish it before she could face Beau again.

"Please, Mom, I want to get up now!"

She seethed at the sound of his voice. It couldn't be far enough away or behind enough doors.

What more do I have to say?

The wine was gone in no time and she collided with the walls as she made the long journey back to the bathroom. She pushed the door open with a bang and Beau sat up on the toilet, watching her with uncertainty. His limp legs dangled pathetically and his red, moist eyes showed how weak he was.

She stood as still as possible and swayed in her drunkenness. Her hands were on her hips and her breathing was heavy.

"Can't you give me any time to do something for myself? Didn't you hear me when I told you that you were going to have to wait?"

"Yes," he said, his fear palpable.

"Did you think I was asking or telling?"

"You were telling me."

"Yeah, I was telling you. So why are you sitting there screaming for me?"

"You waited until I was done and needed your help. You left me sitting here on purpose."

"Yes, I did it to teach you a lesson."

"I don't understand the lesson, Mom."

"That you can't expect me to be around for you like I'm an alarm clock that can be set."

"I had to use the bathroom and you won't let me go without you," he said.

Cailean lunged forward, slow and sloppy in her execution, and slapped him in the face. He reared and fell from the toilet. Clinging to the vanity and the rim of the toilet with arms that trembled from the strain, he grunted and bared his teeth as he tried to hold on.

"Mom?"

His hands were slowly slipping and a look of desperation widened his eyes.

"Please, help me!"

Cailean saw the impression of her fingers on his cheek and the panic on his face registered. In that instant, the seriousness of the situation sobered her and she thrust into action. She lifted Beau back onto the bowl and he felt heavier than when she first helped him out of his chair and placed him on the floor.

Beau rubbed his tired arms and panted. "You hit me," he said.

"And you continue to push me. What do you expect me to do?

"You tried to knock me down," he said and rubbed his face.

She stood upright, his accusation hurtful and untrue.

"I hit you because you have a fresh mouth," she said. "If I wanted to knock you off of the damn toilet, I would have. You can thank me for my help. I could have left you there and watched you fall."

He looked away. "Can you get me into my chair now?"

She nodded. "I suppose, but first, I would like an apology from you for the way you talk back to me. I didn't invite you over so you could bark orders at me and turn me into your servant. You're very foolish. You may be able to talk to your father that way, but you can't talk to me like that."

"I told you I could do it myself."

"You see? You're a smart ass, Beau."

"I want to call Dad," he said. "I don't want to be here anymore."

"I'm fine with that. In fact, I was thinking exactly the same thing. I may be your mother, but now I know that we have nothing in common."

She wanted to lash out and smack him again and again for being so disrespectful but she knew it wouldn't do any good. It would be better if she called Wilson and told him to get Beau out of here.

She reached an arm underneath his legs and placed the other behind his back. She lifted him and teetered. Unable to identify the shift in weight and compensate, she fell forward and tore Beau off of the toilet. Her forehead crashed into the side of the bathtub and filled her head with stars. Landing on top of Beau and unable to feel her body, she pinned him beneath her dead weight and he was trapped, both of them wedged precariously between the bathtub and toilet.

"Mom," he said, his voice dull.

She could hear him but couldn't respond. The blackness was closing in around her and she tried to fight it.

"Please, get off of me . . . I can't breathe," he said.

And no matter how hard she tried, she couldn't move; her body felt like a million pounds and her head throbbed. She could feel his breathing becoming more and more restricted and he started to panic. Pulling at her clothes he fought with desperation, but they were firmly locked.

Blood trickled from the gash on her forehead, rolled down her nose and dripped on his face, going into his eyes, nose and mouth.

The phone rang and the answering machine picked up after several long, drawn out rings. Cailean could hear Wilson instructing her to pick up the phone, and she tried to answer, but the darkness pulled her in.

25

THE PROPOSAL

Present day.

"That is why you threw me down to the ground and had that weight press down on me," Cailean said. "You did it so I would know what it felt like."

"Yes," Sariel said, his voice no longer awful or threatening in any way, but compassionate.

"You're not any of those horrible things I called you," she said.

The meaning behind the messages Sariel had sent were profound. The complexity in which he used to present them brought her to tears. Finally the cry had come and it was real and long overdue.

For the first time she saw things clearly. Everything that happened to Beau, the hell Wilson had to endure, and the emotional rollercoaster ride she brought Emerson on was her fault. The tears she shed were for them and so many others that had fallen victim to her evil.

She felt liberated because she was finally free from what plagued her for so long. And yet the responsibility she felt for the things she had done soured the moment.

"Now that you know what you've done the time has come for you to choose a door," he said.

"The doors," she whispered. "I almost forgot about them."

The distant look in Beau's eyes continued to shame her. Years of abuse and neglect had deprived him of a childhood and any sense of normalcy. Wilson fought the good fight by keeping her at bay and she resented him for it. She wanted the opportunity to tell him she was wrong. That he was a good father and he should be proud.

"I am tired and no longer wish to serve the people," Sariel said. "I have been feared and blamed since the first death and my desire to serve the people no longer burns."

Cailean tried to imagine how it would feel if everyone in the world feared and blamed you for their fast approaching, inevitable demise. The idea of having to face them all and to feel their abhorrence was unthinkable.

"I have grown tired of my endless task and seek nothing more than a reprieve," Sariel said. "I would be pardoned of my duties by your acceptance of my offer."

"How would my acceptance pardon you of your duty?"

"I've had since the creation of sin to think of ways to get myself out of here," he said. "The schemes I have considered would amaze you. But when you came along, you offered me something good, and it was something no one in the entire world ever offered me before."

"What have I offered you?" she said, surprised. "What use could my life give anyone?"

"A way out," he said. "My existence, like the angel that was trapped inside of you, has become torturous. And although your angel died, she left behind so much unshared love that I thought you would be compelled to right your wrongs. Wouldn't you like a chance to have your final message in life to be one of profound love?"

"Yes," she said.

"In exchange for your taking my place, I will give you twenty-four hours of life so you can try and right some of your wrongs. If you agree to this, I will give Beau his life back."

She whimpered. "Beau would get his life back?"

"He would get it back."

"And I get a day to say my peace?"

"I will keep you alive for twenty-four hours."

She nodded. "OK, I'll do it."

"Do you understand what you are accepting?"

She looked at Beau. "Yes, I do."

"It cannot be undone."

"I accept your offer without hesitation or regret. Either way, my life is over, and I now know that this is the only way I'll be able to prove my love for him."

"Very well," Sariel said and stepped into the light.

Cailean looked at him and he towered over her. A long black silk robe covered his body, and a deep, loose fitting hood revealed no part of his face.

"I shall usher your son back to his body and then come back for you. And when your life expires on the other side, you will be thrust into my role, adored by few and feared by many. You will change into what I am with hardly a memory of who you were and what you did. Your only purpose will be to serve the dead."

She looked at Beau and saw him playing with Rafi. He was an innocent victim and deserved her sympathy and sacrifice.

"That doesn't change my decision," she said. "I am ready."

"Then our time is done here," Sariel said.

"What was behind the other door?"

"For you? Hell, I presume. I've never seen inside it and have never had anyone return from it. I believe you have made a great sacrifice and you've redeemed yourself. It appears as though my assessment of you and your angel were correct, and for that I am grateful. But, as I said in the beginning, I have no sympathy for you and I believe you deserve what you will experience in your final hours."

He reached inside his robe and pulled out another black box and set it on the table, this one about half the size of the others.

"There is no reason for you to open this one now," he said. "But you will need to open it once you return here."

26

STACKED CHAOS

The Past.

Wilson's car hit a patch of ice and slid. The vehicle turned sideways and he tried to compensate by steering into the skid. Momentum had turned the car around, and it continued to drift down the road backwards.

Colliding with a hardened pile of snow left behind by the street plows, the car came to a sudden halt and stalled. He started the car again and tried to free it from the frozen trap, but the wheels spun.

He got out of the car and looked to see the rear-end was lodged in the snow; the engine threatened to stall again and dark smoke bellowed out of the hidden tailpipe.

Something inside Wilson nudged him, told him to leave the car and move fast, that Beau needed his help. Three houses away from Cailean's condo, he could see her car was parked in the driveway and already covered by a thick layer of snow.

When he arrived at the front door, he pounded his ungloved fist on the hard wooden door. His lungs burned from the sprint and the cold had a bite that had already numbed his face and hands.

"Cailean," he said and pounded the door again, this time with much more force. "Open the door now or I'm coming in!"

A few seconds felt like forever and the consequences if he might be wrong didn't matter. He rammed his shoulder into the door several times, but his footing slipped and took away much of his power. Backing up a step, he planted a foot on the door just below the doorknob.

Crunch.

The door buckled inwards slightly but still held on. Running into it one last time, it gave way and Wilson fell into the house and onto the floor. Splintered wood debris was scattered all around and when he stood, the silence that he encountered filled him with dread. The sound of his forced entry had unquestionably gained the attention of the neighbors, and yet neither Cailean nor Beau attempted to make contact with him.

"Cailean!"

He listened to the whistle of the wind forcing its way into the house.

"Beau!"

He moved through the living room with wide eyes looking for any sign of what might have happened. The empty wine bottles that were left on the counter brought out an instant, explosive anger.

"Damn it, Cailean, what have you done?"

He hurried his search through the house and glanced over the bare walls and around the plain rooms.

"Cailean?"

He saw the partially closed bathroom door and tried to push it open. Cailean's limp legs acted as a barricade and Wilson forced them out of the way with a hefty push. Cailean was face down on top of Beau, pinning him perilously between the toilet and tub and they both appeared devoid of life.

"Cailean," Wilson said, and grabbed her ankles and pulled. She didn't budge and felt so incredibly heavy. "You need to get off of him."

"What happened?" a voice from somewhere behind Wilson said.

Wilson looked at Emerson standing at the end of the hallway. He was bundled in winter garb and he kept his distance.

"Cailean has fallen on top of Beau! Please, come and help me get her off of him!"

"I can't," Emerson said. "There's not enough room in there for the both of us."

"Then call 9-1-1 and tell them that we need an ambulance," Wilson said.

"Is anyone hurt?"

"I don't know . . . I think so . . . I can't tell, but I need you to call an ambulance. This is bad."

Emerson took his phone out of his pocket and moved out of Wilson's sight.

"I need you to wake up, Cailean," Wilson said. He grabbed her by the ankles again and pulled, but she didn't dislodge. He looked between the toilet and bathtub to see if he could identify what kept her so firmly in place.

The smell of alcohol was overpowering and there was blood pooling on the floor around the bodies. Unsure who it was coming from, Wilson struggled to formulate a plan that would untangle the bodies.

Desperate, he placed a foot on the toilet and grabbed Cailean's shoulders. He pulled up with all of his might and her body bent awkwardly as she lifted off of Beau. The blood made it slippery and she fell from his grasp, tipping to the side and hitting her head on the tile floor. A new gash hidden underneath her hair started to gush.

"Beau," Wilson said and hovered over him, afraid to touch. Blood that painted his face and pooled around his head didn't appear as though it had come from him. His lips were purple and his face a ghostly white, frozen in the final moments of his struggle to break free.

"I don't want to move you, son. Help is on the way," Wilson said. "Just hang on."

"The ambulance," Emerson said. "They're on their way."

Wilson found it curious that Emerson kept a certain distance, but Beau and Cailean's conditions were more pressing. He examined the lump across her forehead and it looked bad. Streams of blood that had poured from the gaping slit in the center of the bump had run down her face and dripped off of her chin. Swelling bloated her face and the rise and fall of her chest was subtle.

"If you're not going to help me," Wilson shouted, "then I want you to leave!"

The flash of anger took away his control.

Emerson stopped pacing and looked at Wilson.

"We had a bit of a falling out," Emerson said. "She seemed edgy and told me to leave. I came back because I was concerned."

"Concerned?"

"About what she might do," Emerson said.

"Come and see. Look at what she's done!"

Wilson stormed out of the bathroom and marched down the hallway; blood stained his hands and clothes.

Emerson backed away from the much smaller man.

"How could you let this happen?" Wilson said.

"I didn't know."

"You knew enough to come here and check on her?"

"I—"

"I swear, if I find out you had something to do with this, I'll kill you."

Wilson seethed. This man was just another part of Cailean's problems. He allowed her to do what she wanted and even encouraged it.

He turned to walk away to care for his family. But he noticed the wine bottles that were on the counter were now gone. He looked at Emerson.

"The bottles of wine, what did you do with them?"

"What bottles of wine?" he said. "What are you talking about?"

Wilson screamed out in anger and charged at Emerson. He shoved him back and slammed him into the wall. He held onto his coat and shook him.

"You know exactly what I'm talking about! What did you do with the bottles?"

"All right," Emerson said and raised his hands in surrender. "I threw them away."

Wilson loosened his grip. "Why would you do that?"

"Because I'm the one who gave them to her, OK? I didn't mean for this to happen. She was supposed to drink them after Beau left. She wasn't even supposed to drink both of them."

"Where did you dispose of them?"

"Outside. I threw them in a mound of snow because I don't want to look at them."

"With that going on in there," he pointed at the bathroom, "that is what you think of? Covering your tracks?"

"I feel responsible for what happened in there."

"There's something more to your guilt. Why else would you think to do that? It's in you like it's in Cailean."

Emerson shook his head. "No, it's in my daughter. I believed if I could fix Cailean, or even understand her, then maybe I could help my daughter."

"Help your daughter with what?" Wilson said.

"I don't know what it is. That day at the park, the day Beau got hurt, Cailean was drunk, but she didn't do anything wrong except meet me. My daughter shoved your son off of the playground. I think she was showing her anger towards me for talking to another woman when her mother was dead. I'm so confused."

Emerson's admission immersed Wilson in a whirlwind of many different emotions that he got lost in them. Maybe he was too hard on Cailean, and maybe he should have listened to her more.

"I can't live with that secret anymore," Emerson said. "I am dead on the inside and you deserve to know the truth before I leave this earth."

Paramedics rushed into the house.

"Where are they?"

"They're at the end of the hallway, in the bathroom," Emerson said, and he walked past Wilson. "I'm sorry about everything," he said, and exited the house.

27

A LIFE UNWORTHY

Present day.

Emerson examined the wall over the doorjamb. He had cut a hole through the sheetrock, slung a rope over the doorframe and wrapped it around the thick supports. A noose that hung in the middle of the doorway swung menacingly, retelling him what he was about to do could not be undone. He dumped a cup of water on the floor directly beneath the snare. Emerson felt like he was standing at the gallows and had the burden of answering whether or not he had any last words to say.

"Please comfort me in my time of need," he prayed, and wiped the sweat from his brow. His hands were tense and had a steady tremble that made it difficult to handle the rope. He managed to place the noose around his neck and make it as tight as possible.

Placing handcuffs around each wrist, he moved his hands behind his back and joined them together. He tested the restraints by trying to pull his hands apart. The cuffs held tight, digging into his skin. The idea of keeping his hands tethered behind his back in case he panicked came upon him in a dream.

Inhuman things with encouraging voices came to him often and convinced him that his death would be better for everyone. That he was responsible for the bad seed inside of his daughter, for the demise of his wife and Cailean's suffering. When he tried to resist the monsters, they would surround him and growl, their sharp teeth menacing, their breath beating and horrible.

Night after night he was confronted by these things, losing sleep and unable to resist their commands. Last night they had told him that if he was to tie his hands behind his back he wouldn't be able to undo it and his torment would end.

Now he knew they were right. Everything that happened to him over the past several years had brought him to this moment. The death of his wife, the mental breakdown his child suffered, and the obligation he felt towards Cailean and Beau because of what he saw his daughter do at the park. The way she baited Beau to the top of the playground and shoved him off made him realize he had lost his daughter the same day he lost his wife. When she died, the better part of Stacey left with her, never to return.

For months he tried to live with the repercussions from that day at the park. He tolerated behavior he normally wouldn't stand for, and even became a part of it. But witnessing what his daughter's touch and his own presence had done to Cailean and her family in that bathroom became too painful to bear.

People died because of us. This family is cursed and I can only wonder what sins I've inherited.

Something inside of his daughter was evil and he couldn't understand how to reason with it. Neither could his wife, and they didn't acknowledge it until Stacey was around the age of five. After a year of counseling Stacey's behavior continued to worsen and it had proven to be too much for his wife.

"Christina, bless your heart," Emerson said. "It wasn't your fault."

Christina had walked into the family room where he watched television and Stacey played with her dolls.

"You didn't come from me," Christina had said to Stacey. Immediately after, she stuck a gun in her mouth, her eyes crazed, and she pulled the trigger.

"But I know you're better off," Emerson said. "That was no way for you to live. And Stacey?"

He smiled.

"You're better off where you are now," he said. "They will care for you in Sunnyside Capable Care. The institution is known for its extraordinary care, and I have provided them with enough money to care for you over the course of your entire life."

She appeared to be taking a liking to Doctor Anna Lee. He noticed the bond that had been formed at the park. That was the first time she allowed anyone to get that close to her since her mother's death.

Emerson was glad they were able to take her to the park, but was saddened by the outcome. He couldn't get himself to tell Doctor Lee what had happened or show her the picture he took. It was the one of Stacey holding Beau's hand and leading him around the playground. When he first examined the picture and saw his daughter looking back at him with pure evil he didn't know what to do.

He hid the picture and didn't look at it again until today. Compelled to make fifty copies, he taped them all over the walls.

The time for reminiscing had come to an end.

"I now understand why you ended your life, Christina," he said. "I saw what you must've seen and I cannot live with that."

He clamped his eyes shut, and said, "Forgive me for what I must do."

He dropped to his knees and all three hundred pounds of him stopped with a forceful jerk. The noose cinched around his neck and the rope whined. The flesh tore and oozed blood and an immense amount of pressure on the inside of his head made it feel as though his eyes were being pushed out of their sockets.

The instinct to survive took over and he struggled to find his footing, but his feet slipped on the wet floor. He tried to lift his hands, but the handcuffs kept his wrists bound behind his back. He tried to draw breath but couldn't.

Sariel had seen enough. He reached his hand out and dragged his fingernails across the rope. It frayed and snapped. Emerson fell to the floor with a heavy thump. The noose remained tight around his neck and he gurgled as he tried to breathe in.

"Yes," Sariel said. "This is going to be a long and painful death for you."

Emerson's soul reached for Sariel, desperate to part from its failing vessel.

"No, I won't take this away from her," Sariel said. "Twenty-four hours and Cailean will come for you. I want to make sure you are the first soul she escorts to the door. Although she won't recognize you, you will beg her for forgiveness for what you have done to her family."

28

A MIRACLE

Present day.

Wilson rested his elbows on his knees and watched the steady rise and fall of Beau's chest tucked firmly beneath the bed sheets. A machine monitored his vitals like a relentless guard keeping constant vigil over his frail son. The beeping sounds were a welcomed distraction. Often he found himself staring at the display of the beating heart that showed the steady rhythm of Beau's pulse.

Though Beau was very pale and clammy, he had shown great improvement over the past twelve hours. Wilson remained optimistic that his son would emerge from his brush with death with no lasting effects.

Tubes and wires that were hooked to his small body took away waste and fed him intravenously. Purple bruises surrounded his closed eyes. The doctor said it was from the broken nose he suffered when Cailean landed on top of him.

Wilson reached out and took hold of Beau's cold, limp hand. Welts stained the skin on his forearm and the top of his hand. What Wilson saw implored his scrutiny.

Beau's fingernails were split and oozing—a direct sign of his struggle to free himself.

Wilson couldn't help but imagine the horror his son went through as his mother fell on top of him and pinned him to the floor. Wilson kept mentally placing himself beneath Cailean's weight to try to comprehend what he might have gone through.

A surge of anger came over him and he stifled a scream.

"I couldn't imagine what you were thinking," he said, and squeezed Beau's hand. "I could only imagine how horrible that must have been for you."

He surmised that Beau pushed and clawed at the floor as he tried to get himself out from beneath someone many times heavier than his own body weight. The thing that bothered Wilson the most was that Beau didn't have the use of his legs to help gain leverage and increase his chance of escaping.

"I should never have given in to my desire to have us all back together as a happy, functioning family again. I knew I needed to keep her away from you, but for my own selfish reasons even I don't understand, I risked placing you in harm's way."

When he was outside with Cailean after she showed up uninvited, deep down inside his sense of right and wrong screamed at him. It told him not to allow her anywhere near Beau, that she couldn't be trusted. But the idea that he could save her from the ghosts of her past and instill a moral compass for her to steer by had become his own addiction.

"Please," Wilson prayed. "He has been through so much."

The memory of the treating physician was murky because of shock and disbelief, and yet he remembered the look of concern that poked through his professional demeanor, and that unnerved Wilson.

"I am uncertain as to the long-term effects this will have on your son," the doctor had said. "I want you to understand that he was oxygen deprived for a long time. But right now I need to focus my efforts on keeping him stable."

Cailean had arrived at the hospital around the same time as Beau, barely clinging to life. He knew very little about her current condition. The head trauma she suffered had been gruesome and difficult to look at. He didn't need a doctor to tell him how bad it was.

"My life for his," Wilson said, and felt the offer was reasonable. He closed his eyes and hoped with all of his being that the sincerity of his request meant something. He squeezed Beau's hand again.

"Please, God, I'm begging you to show your mercy. I believe in you and the miracles you can make happen."

Beau opened his eyes and struggled to focus on a soundless television perched high on the wall. He was lying on his back in a soft bed and heavy blankets covered him. A bright overhead light shined down on him and hurt his eyes.

"My life for his."

The voice that just uttered those words sounded so sad. A gentle, desperate squeeze on his right hand made him fight against the incredible heaviness that settled in his head and he managed to look at his father.

"Please, I'm begging you to show your mercy," his father said. "I believe in you and the miracles you can make happen."

Beau licked his lips and drew a deep breath. His chest was sore, but the heart that beat beneath the bruises longed to comfort the man that loved and cared for him unconditionally.

"Dad?" Beau said and the strain made him cough.

Wilson stood up fast, his face bright with surprise and doubt. He stared at Beau, wordless.

"Who are you talking to?" Beau said.

"I've been speaking to God and to you," he said and tears brightened his eyes. His face threw off messages of pure delight and a moment later, pure confusion.

"I heard everything you said. About how you would give your life for mine."

"I would do it if that is what it takes."

"I know that, Dad. I love you, too."

Wilson couldn't maintain his composure. He leaned on the bed and gave in to the cry.

"Dad, are you OK?"

"Yes, son, I'm fine."

"Then why are you crying?"

"I'm just happy you're awake and that I'm able to talk to you."

"Where am I, Dad? What is this place?"

"You're in the hospital. You were in a terrible accident."

"I remember Mom falling on top of me."

He nodded. "Yes, she did, Beau."

"She hit her head on the bathtub and was bleeding really bad."

"I know, son."

"I could taste it," he said and licked his lips. "I think I still can."

"I'll ask them to give you something to help get rid of the taste."

"Where is she?" Beau said and tried to sit up.

"No," Wilson said and encouraged him back down with a gentle hand on his shoulder. "Don't do that. You have to stay in bed."

"Where is Mom?"

Wilson's eyes overflowed with tears and he stroked Beau's hair. "She's in a different room down the hall from where we are and the doctors are looking after her."

"I couldn't get her off of me. She was so heavy and it was really hard for me to breathe. I remember you calling and talking into the answering machine, and I even answered you, but you couldn't hear me."

"I know, son, and I'm sorry. I will always be there for you from now on."

"You have always been there for me."

"Not when it mattered most."

"How did you know?"

"I came over as fast as I could. I knew something had to be wrong when the phone kept going to the answering machine."

"You found Mom on top of me?"

"Yes."

Beau sat in silence, and soon said, "I know this is going to sound crazy to you, Dad, but I saw mom just before I woke up. She was talking to me."

His father kissed him on the forehead.

"We were underneath a bright light together," he said and pointed to the fixture over his bed. "It was a lot like this one, only it was much brighter. She didn't have any hair and seemed really sad."

"Shh," Wilson said and touched Beau's lips. "I need you to try and get some rest."

"No, Dad," he said and propped himself up with his elbows. "What I am telling you was real. She was talking to someone that was outside the lighted area and she was making a deal with him. She gave her life for mine. She cried a lot and told me how sorry she was. And before I was taken away from her she told me that she loved me."

"I know she loves you, Beau. I've never doubted that, not once."

"I remember it snowing there but it wasn't cold at all. I could hear everything they were saying but I can't remember most of it. It was like I was in a dream, only it was real."

"Please, you need to rest," Wilson said.

Beau felt the gentle press of his father's hand as he encouraged him to lay flat again.

"I have to let the nurses know you're awake," Wilson said.

Wilson pressed the call button on the side of Beau's bed, summoning a nurse.

"Wait," Beau said and lifted the blanket and searched for something hidden there. "Mom gave me something before I left the light."

Just then, a nurse entered the room and took notice of Beau. "He's awake? I need to get the doctor right away."

"Dad?"

Wilson looked at him.

He held Rafi up for his father to see.

"This is what she gave me."

Wilson's mouth hung open and he slowly reached out and took Rafi from Beau's hands.

"How is that even possible? I haven't left your side."

"I told you, Mom gave it to me."

"Nurse?" Wilson shouted, and a moment later she returned.

"Did you or someone on your staff bring this in to him?"

"No," she said.

"Oh," Wilson said. "OK, thank you."

"Is that all? I should get the doctor."

"Yeah," he said.

She hurried out of the room.

"And, Dad," Beau said. "There is something else."

He pointed at the foot of his bed and wiggled his toes.

Wilson kissed Beau. "I love you son."

"I love you, too, Dad."

He let go of Beau's hand and watched a nurse wheel him down the hallway.

"His recovery is nothing short of a miracle," the treating physician said. "The fact that he has awoken with such awareness is a wonder enough, but the fact that he has feeling in his legs again and is able to move them is simply astounding."

Lost for words, Wilson shook his head in agreement and pure joy swept over him.

"They're going to need to run some tests on him to see if they can find some answers to this."

"I understand."

"But we also need to discuss your wife."

Wilson nodded. "Of course."

"I want you to count your blessings with the miraculous recovery your son has had and understand that he will need your continued support."

He nodded in his continued understanding.

"The trauma your wife has suffered is severe, and I'm afraid I have done all I can do. The swelling on her brain required me to remove the top of her skull. She's slipped into a coma and it is something she will never come out of. I need you to prepare yourself for what is to come and reach out to any family members that you are able to count on. Although she is still alive, she is in a vegetative state and is steadily declining with each passing moment. It is my opinion that she will not live past the night."

Wilson nodded, deeply saddened.

"I'm truly sorry," the doctor said. "If there is anything you need to say to your wife, now might be the time for you to do so."

"I'm sorry you had such a hard life," Wilson said, standing over the bed Cailean was in. Her breathing was more like a raspy gargle. He sat next to her and rubbed her arm.

"I was really scared when I found you on top of Beau. I didn't know what to do. And all that blood . . ."

He shook his head at the memory and saw her nail beds were turning a blackish purple. He checked her feet and they were also turning color, and he knew from his father's passing that death was entering her body.

"Right after I found you, Emerson stopped by to check on you at the house. He told me that he was in a relationship with you because he felt guilty. He said that his daughter was responsible for Beau falling off of the playground, not you. She pushed Beau out of jealousy. He said there was something emotionally wrong with his daughter. And for that, I'm sorry I was so hard on you."

Her face was wrapped with a thick layer of gauze and her eyes rested easy.

"Maybe you can hear me. I don't know. Beau believes he saw you on the other side and that you gave up your life for him. If that is true, I want you to know that he came back to me."

Wilson took Cailean's hand into his own and he rubbed it gently.

"When he awoke, he pulled Rafi out from under his blankets to prove to me he was with you. It sounds crazy, I know, but it's the truth. I wouldn't have believed it if I didn't see it with my own eyes."

A tear rolled down Cailean's cheek and Wilson wiped it away.

"But the most amazing thing is he wiggled his toes. I think the accident somehow fixed his spine. But if you did have something to do with this, thank you, it's the best present you could ever give him."

Wilson began to cry. The tears were for her and the tragic events that brought them together and split them apart. They were for Beau and the possibility that he might walk again someday. And lastly, because he knew this was his goodbye to her. As difficult and chaotic as she had made his life, he really loved her.

"Go on," he said and placed a gentle kiss on her cheek. "Rest in peace."

Cailean could hear everything Wilson said to her, but no matter how hard she tried, she couldn't respond. There were so many things she wanted to say before she died, but her lips were as heavy as bricks and she no longer had command over her voice.

Panic filled her body and wrapped her tightly, proving its might was much stronger than her will.

She realized that she had been tricked.

Sariel made a promise to give her twenty-four hours of life to try and right her wrongs. His promise has been fulfilled. She was still alive, but unable to communicate.

She was certain that this is what he meant when he told her she deserved what she would experience in her final hours. Because she wanted nothing more than to say two little words that meant so much now.

29

THE LAST BLACK BOX

Present day.

Cailean stood naked beneath a light that hurt her eyes. For some reason, she peeled black wrapping paper off of a box she had found sitting on a table unattended. She couldn't remember how she got there or where she was. Her thoughts were consumed with the idea that she had left something undone. But the chill all around her distracted her and she moved quickly to extract a neatly folded garment out of the box.

The black robe was as soft as silk, yet somehow heavy, and it offered her protection from the elements. Putting the gown on, she neatened it and raised the hood over her head.

Comfortable from within the black cavity, she peered out; the light above her head buzzed and flickered. Sparks shot from the fixture and the light went out. Immersed in darkness, a distant voice called out to her. Impossible to ignore, she set out on her journey to locate its source. Somehow she knew that during her travels she would have plenty of time to think about what she had left unfinished.

BOOKS BY
KEITH ROMMEL